UNDER
SIEGE

A RICHARD JACKSON
BOOK

UNDER SIEGE

ELISABETH MACE

ORCHARD BOOKS

New York

Orchard Books
A division of Franklin Watts, Inc.
387 Park Avenue South
New York, NY 10016

Manufactured in the United States
of America. Book design by
Mina Greenstein. The text of this
book is set in 12 pt. Fournier
10 9 8 7 6 5 4 3 2 1

Library of Congress Cataloging-in-
Publication Data
Mace, Elisabeth.
Under siege / Elisabeth Mace.—
1st American ed.
p.   cm. "A Richard Jackson book."
Summary: Unable to change events
dealing with his parent's separation,
Morris gets the chance to play God
when the characters of his com-
puter fantasy game come to life.
ISBN 0-531-05871-9.
ISBN 0-531-08471-X (lib. bdg.)
[1. Computer games—Fiction.
2. Fantasy games—Fiction.
3. Family problems—Fiction.]
I. Title.
PZ7.M15845Un   1990
[Fic]—dc20   89-23049   CIP   AC

Acknowledgments

Grateful acknowledgment for the idea
which triggered off this book is made to
Philip K. Dick's story "War Game" from
The Preserving Machine and Other Stories
published by Victor Gollancz Limited.

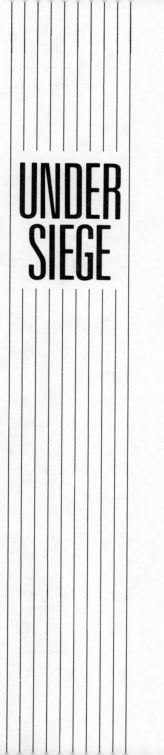

UNDER SIEGE

he car journey took just under two hours.

Morris Nelson and his mother spent the time either in silence or blaming each other and Mr. Nelson for anything that was wrong.

Everything was wrong.

They were long past the stage of polite pretense when by themselves, though managing slightly better in company. Mr. Nelson was not with them. He hadn't been with them for most of the past year. Among other things, Morris was blaming his mother for whipping him out of school before the end of term, school being preferable to home. They were going to spend a long Christmas and New Year with her brother Patrick, who still lived in her family home territory. Morris said he would rather have stayed in their empty house, alone.

His mother answered that at length. A lot about girls or worse and being responsible for him even if his father wasn't. Morris didn't listen. She probably knew he didn't listen, but once wound up, couldn't stop. The phrase "your father" riddled her discourse like scattered shot.

Morris told her to watch her driving. They relapsed into silence.

He thought he'd never been to the brother's house, and it was a long time since he'd visited any other relations here. His mother had been several times recently, but so full of woe and rage against her wicked husband that she'd willingly left Morris at home. Then it was: "At sixteen, Morris, you can see to yourself." Now it was: "Sixteen's too young to spend Christmas by yourself."

Brother Patrick apparently—though a bachelor—lived in a large house called East Lodge in the middle of nowhere. The side road to get there soon faded into a muddy track. The house itself was shapeless and dishonest; bits built on or fallen down, patched and repainted. Several upper windows were boarded over; creeper had been pulled off the roof and left hanging to rot or reassert itself.

"I hope," Mrs. Nelson said disloyally, "Patrick has at least shifted himself to air us a couple of rooms."

"He's got enough, by the looks of it," Morris observed.

His mother sighed heavily and told him to take his case and bundled-up sleeping bag.

"Doesn't he have beds?" Morris asked.

She didn't answer.

It took three buzzes and a long silence before anyone came to the door. Morris was almost beginning to enjoy himself, it was so awful. "Does he know we're coming?" he asked. Again, she didn't answer.

2   Patrick helped with the luggage because he was in

a hurry to get the door shut again. There were no family kisses or foolish greetings. It was as if they'd just been out shopping.

"Here's Morris," his mother said. Patrick nodded and led the way upstairs. "I do think you could get some new stair carpet; this is a deathtrap," she went on. "Is the house dry, Patrick? I hope it's dry."

"Good God, woman," he muttered, swinging the luggage he carried at a long radiator, "how could I run my setups if it wasn't?"

"Well, how should I know what you're up to these days? From the look of the place outside it'd best suit fungus farming."

"Look—" Patrick went into a room without warning—"if you don't like it, Annie, leave it. I don't tell you how to run your house. This is mine, all right? You can sleep in here and Morris across there." Then he left them to decide.

In Morris's room there was a bed with basic covers, a chair, a bedside lamp (on the floor), and an old chest with three drawers. When his mother came to see, he asked, "Is he poor, your brother?" He couldn't think or speak of him as "uncle"—besides, the man wasn't that old, possibly thirty; hard to tell. *How will he treat me? Does he know I'm not a kid?*

"Poor? Those radiators blasting away, probably never off?" A bitter laugh. "He doesn't know how to spend his money, that's all."

"But you moaned in case the house was damp," Morris pointed out.

For answer she threw back the sheet and sole blan- 3

ket on the bed. "Where's your sleeping bag? I knew you'd need it. Now we'd better see if there's anything to eat in this godforsaken place."

Morris said, "Why did we come? I told you I wanted to stay at home."

"Oh, not again. . . ."

The food, like the central heating, was a surprise. They were introduced to a vast, well-stocked freezer, a stove, and a microwave, and invited to help themselves. "Forget about me," Patrick said. "I eat when I feel like it, and anyway I'll be at work most of the time. There's tea, coffee, all that stuff in those cupboards. Look, I have to go out now, I'll see you later, all right?"

She went after him, but had no chance.

Morris started rummaging merrily in the depths of the freezer. His mother said crossly, "What are you singing for? What a way to live—a fortune in frozen food and electricity, and furnishings left over from a garage sale. No wonder he never married, no woman would—"

"Which ought to make him a saint, according to you."

"All men are idiots."

"Me as well?"

"*You.* Get out of my way, Morris. My God, look at that revolting cutlery, does the man never wash up?"

"When you're finished," Morris said, "I'll come and see to myself; I'm used to it." And he wandered off, feeling for light switches in strange rooms, since no one had told him not to. He could admire Patrick already.

He found one room with armchairs and a huge, dented sofa opposite a TV and a VCR. There were technical magazines, booze bottles, and dirty glasses abandoned across the floor. He had a sudden urge to hide the bottles from his mother. The magazines were quite unreadable. Even the covers were dull. He thought they were to do with computers; or maybe not. Several magazines were in a foreign language— German? Swedish? Among them were pieces of paper covered with unintelligible diagrams and sets of numbers.

His mother came to announce food. She winced at the sight of the room but didn't comment.

They ate quickly, in silence. Then Mrs. Nelson said, "Now Morris, I'm going to drive over to see Della" (her sister). "We can't be doing with all *this*."

Morris reminded her, "But you said Della couldn't put us up."

"Right. I'm only going to *see* her; she might—I can't be doing with this." She gazed hopelessly around. "Just wash up while I'm gone. Please."

"But why? Patrick never does."

"We don't have to follow that example."

"How long will you be?"

"Oh I don't know; you'd better take yourself off to bed when you're ready, we're stuck here tonight. And Morris, don't go poking into your uncle's things. I don't know whatever made me think we could stay here."

5

"What things?"

"Oh I don't know, he's always had crazes, building things, running things; there'll be a roomful of it somewhere. Some people never grow up." She drew breath. "Anyway, you hear me; whatever he's playing with now, just leave it alone. And do that washing up."

She was gone. He swilled the things under hot water and left them to drain. There wouldn't be a dish towel anyway.

Then he began to search the house. How could they expect otherwise?

There were cellars, well-lit but uninviting, things covered with plastic sheeting, a couple of old bikes, more booze. The ground floor was already explored: piled-up boxes in one room, too heavy and well packed to investigate.

Upstairs. His mother's room, his room, bathroom, a tiny empty room, another bedroom (probably Patrick's) around a surprise corner. More stairs; narrower, bare-boarded. More rooms. The first and second doors were locked. Only the last of the three gave to his hand. Something told Morris that if two doors out of three in a row were locked, he ought to leave it, but he was already pushing the door wide open into the pitch-black room.

There was no need to seek a switch. The opening door must have activated the low, cold light which gradually brightened like a winter dawn. The windows had been boarded up, the walls between this room and the two beyond knocked out. The space within was another world, a complete landscape with fields, rocks, trees, small buildings, pathways ... and off center, rising above all, a great castle. In the cunning light, the ceiling and enclosing walls had disappeared: Morris was a giant in a new yet very ancient country.

2

At once he leaned his back against the door to close it: the light faded into rapid night. So the door must stay open; so much the easier to hear footsteps below.

He edged with slow care down the room. He wanted to approach the castle, to touch its clever walls that looked just like real stone; to measure its height above his own; to peer over the battlements and see if the marvelous detail continued within, or was just a hollow sham—oh surely not—he wanted to, but didn't dare. The floor of the room had been modeled and transformed so cunningly into a country landscape, he was afraid of the unknown harm his huge feet would cause. Yet there must be a way—his uncle, who had presumably constructed all this himself, would surely never be content just to stare at that glorious castle from a distance.

Morris moved slowly on down the room, feeling the wall at his back; past one locked door and then the other. Now the castle presented quite a different view of itself, as if it were on a raised escarpment, with rocks beneath; a narrow road leading from its closed gates down into the empty land and winding away through woods stretching behind and along the outside length of the room.

The trees, too, looked uncommonly real. Perhaps they were those Japanese bonsai trees, cultivated to stay deliberately miniature. Morris knelt down and dared to touch the nearest tree, a twisted conifer growing from a rock fissure. A tiny pine needle pricked his finger and there was a brief scent of Christmas. The tree's mother-rock was cold in its early morning light. Beneath the rock were grainy stones and moorland grass. Morris pinched a tuft between thumb and finger. As he felt the resistance of its roots, he pushed it back with his nail and shuddered.

Then he saw, between scrub and trees, a lone building, a small hutlike construction of stone and wood, with a pitched, thatched roof of turf. *A woodman's hovel, maybe.* Since it was close enough to the outer boundary (*border-country,* thought Morris) he was able to contrive himself so as to peer single-eyed in through the spyhole of a window.

He could see: a rough table and by it two stools, utensils on an open shelf, a bed-place, and—frustratingly almost out of view—a single standing figure. To see it better would mean lying down before the only other window. And that would mean flattening a couple of trees and a length of stone wall. Morris wondered if he might insert a hand, draw out the little figure to have a look, then put it back again. Who would know?

Looking for the best approach, he noticed another

9

figure deep among the trees. Morris shifted his position for a closer view, though the model was well camouflaged, stippled like woodland shade and in either a sitting or crouching pose. *Hiding,* he thought, *or watching. Both, probably, for this whole setup must be for some gigantic game. In which case, there must be many more model people, perhaps all stowed away in the castle, or lined up in formation down the side I haven't seen yet.*

It was like being five years old again, in the age of Santa Claus. Uncannily like. As he was lying low, head on the floor, eyes at model level, so he remembered lying once, slowly pushing a toy vehicle across his vision and making soft engine noises in his throat.

He raised himself a little and crept along, outside the wood, watching all the time for more delights. Every minute or so he put his head to the ground again, to peer between the trees. Each time, the view had changed, but there were no more tiny people.

This time he could see a definite forest track. It was as if he was standing on it, gazing through to the open road and, beyond that, the very wall of the castle. And there were bird sounds, tinnily distant, surely in his head, and—music? Brave music, from the castle.

Then a voice said, "Well?"

He sat up, dazed.

At the end of the room it had sadly shrunk into, his uncle and another man were observing his confusion.

"What do you think?" Patrick asked.

"I didn't touch anything," Morris lied, hoping the little conifer wouldn't wither and die.

"Good. Do you like it?"

"It's magnificent, it's—" He shook his head. "I don't know how to say it."

"Forget it. Good job you didn't touch. Don't."

"No, of course not."

"Unless I say so. You want to see?"

Morris nodded, wondering what, not knowing what to hope for.

"Over here. By the way, where's Annie?"

"Mom? She went to see her sister Della, I think."

Patrick grunted. "Right; now watch. Right, Ian, bring up 5."

"Full on?"

"Why not."

Ian, who nodded at Morris first, leaned across him to slide a switch on a large console stacked along the end wall. Morris wondered how he'd missed seeing it earlier. Now he understood what it was all about: construct the layout, wire it up, play about with switches, abracadabra.

Number 5 flooded the scene with clear noonday sunshine. The three observers stood and gave it thought.

Patrick moved along to squint at the castle gates. He called Ian, pointed, and made a comment. Ian flicked a switch which illuminated a screen above the console. More adjustments, until the very bolts which held the great doors shut were in close-up. On the screen, the bolts looked massive, of heavy iron. Ian and Patrick swapped rapid technicalities. Then they viewed the door hinges as well.

"No," Ian said. That was the only word Morris understood.

"What was the last strategy we tried?" Patrick asked. He took up a large file and they sifted through it together, making more quite unintelligible comments all the while.

Morris asked gingerly, "Is it a war game?"

Patrick glanced up. "Sort of. No, not really. A siege, you might say."

"To capture the castle?"

Patrick hummed, more concerned with details, still not satisfied with the security of the main doors.

"Here's the last foray," Ian said, showing a paper. They ran through numbers related to a diagram; probably grid references, Morris thought. It would be like the fantasy games he'd taken part in himself, but on such a grand scale—light-years away from the old board-game style he'd known.

Patrick took the file slowly down the length of the room. At the far end he called, "Give us a view of the farm, D3, and home in."

A building came up on the screen, wall by wall.

"In at that window."

As in the woodman's hut, Morris could see into a room, simply furnished but with more show of comfort; a table set with a number of places, chairs with high backs, a closed cupboard. The attention to detail everywhere was amazing. He wondered what Patrick was looking for.

"Wherever have they—hah!"

They were viewing an upstairs room, a sort of dormitory lined with narrow beds. Unbelievably, each bed contained a sleeping figure; everything—walls, beds, figures, an uncolored milky wash. Probably unpainted, not needed for action. But why was Patrick examining them now? Unless he'd mislaid one; maybe that crouched watcher in the woods.

"All present," Ian said. "Shall we rouse them?"

"Would you like to see a foray?" Patrick asked Morris. "Shall we tickle them up?"

"You bet!"

"What'll it be?" Patrick prowled the perimeter, humming to himself. "We'll leave that lot in bed," he decided. "Those doors still bother me, Ian. Let's see what they've been up to. *Assault from the North*, right?"

"Lighting?" Ian asked.

"Daybreak, fine weather, we might as well *see* the show."

Beneath Ian's hand the bright sun dimmed almost into night, paused, then lightened enough—like a theatrical scene-change—to reveal a set of model figures lined up and waiting on the fringe of the wood facing the castle gates. Morris could have sworn they had not been there a minute before, yet no hand had put them in place. Perhaps it was another light trick, since each tensed little figure was painted to blend in exactly with the coarse gray-green of the terrain. More cunning still, as the dawn light gently lifted to bring out detail and color in the landscape, so the camouflage of the figures seemed to change to match it.

How would they move the pieces? What about the castle?

"Here they come," Patrick murmured.

13

Morris heard again the tinny sound of music from inside the castle, like a toy fife band, out of view. And on the move, too, not a recording set up in a fixed position. He could believe that the band was surely going to appear on the battlements above the gates at any second now.

Then, "How did you do that?" he cried.

The lined-up figures had all moved while his attention was on the castle. Now they were in a widely spaced-out formation at the very foot of the castle's rock foundation. Incredible. And changed yet again, now as dark as the rocks which protected them. They must be holograms—no, that was strictly science fiction.

"They're not going for the doors," Ian said.

"Damn. I wanted to see—" Patrick looked up suddenly, listening. "What's that downstairs?"

Morris knew, and could have wept. "It'll be Mom," he said.

"Is she to join us?"

"No, no!" To leave the game at this point was torture, but to let his mother in was unthinkable.

Ian said, "Shall I shut it down?"

"No, run it through," Patrick said. He nodded at Morris. "Another time, all right? It'll still be here." Meaning, hop it sharp.

As he left, the fife band stopped playing, a lone figure appeared on a high turret, a trumpet sounded, thin and clear, a needle to the heart.

3

"**Y**ou weren't long," Morris said to his mother.

She noted his high color. "Indeed? And what have you been up to?"

"Nothing."

"I warned you, Morris. You might think my brother's not of this world, but just you try crossing him."

"He's upstairs with a friend," Morris said. She glanced upward. "They're busy."

"Doing what? Ah, Morris, your face is an open book. Playing trains? Blowing up the universe? Oh," she turned away, "don't bother to tell stories, I really couldn't care less. It won't matter anyway once we're out of here." She started opening and slamming cupboards, looking for coffee.

"You said your sister Della couldn't have us."

"She's not the only soul I know around here."

Morris waited but she wasn't going to be helpful. He had to prod. "Well, go on."

"More than likely Cousin Bea can take us."

"Who? Where?"

"After tomorrow, there'll be just her and her little girl at their house."

"Where's Mr. B.?"

"Abroad. Now look Morris—"

"I'm not staying in any old nest of women!" he shouted.

"You'll do as you're told, my friend."

"I'll stop here with Patrick. He wouldn't mind."

"And *do what here?*"

They faced each other in the now familiar stance of warfare.

It was Morris's turn. "We're both men," he said. "We can be *idiots* together. He's got the most amazing setup, up there; he's going to show me how to . . ." He couldn't face saying "how to play."

"How to play," his mother obliged.

"You brought me here," Morris pointed out.

"True." She paused, not looking at him. "I can't always think straight," she said. "I had to get us away."

"But you must have known—he is your brother, and you said—"

"I know, I know. Things seem different from seventy—eighty miles away."

"But it's only games, no harm."

"No good either. Now get to bed."

"You treat me like a baby."

"That's exactly what I want to avoid. Playing at games. Get to bed. Please."

End of skirmish. He wanted to go straightway into 16 that forbidden room and bash the unliving daylights out of the whole stupid setup. And all he could do was to sit in his bare bedroom and wonder at the meaning of the sounds above his head. Very muffled, but definitely overhead. *They* must be up there, having a rare old time playing soldiers.

He couldn't bear it. In another breath he was up the narrow stairs and along the passageway past the two locked doors. Three locked doors. Push as he might, the third door stayed fast shut. Oh, how she'd laugh if she knew! And Patrick had seemed so friendly, so willing to share his treasures. (*"Just you try crossing him," she'd warned. Had I? How?*) But the door was locked. They must have heard him trying to get in—he knew they were in there—and no smiling face opened to welcome him back. Humiliated, he went down to his room, from where he could still hear those faint sounds overhead; even, once, a hearty laugh.

| | | | | | | | | | | |

He was awakened in the early morning by voices on the landing:

Patrick saying, "I'm sorry, Annie, but I've got to go to work now."

She saying, "And I'm sorry, but you must see my point of view."

"Any view you like," Patrick agreed, "so long as you're happy."

She protested furiously, but it was clear he'd escaped.

"What about Morris?" the listener heard her cry, but not Patrick's answer, if any.

His mother returned to her room and shut the door,

none too quietly. It wasn't possible now to go back to sleep; nor, he knew, was there anything to read in the bare room, so it wasn't worth putting on the light. At least it wasn't cold in this hothouse. Hot so all those doubtless expensive models didn't grow damp and moldy and unworkable. Morris lay on his back and stared at the ceiling, now gradually becoming visible as the night receded. He saw again in his mind the way the lighting system up there could reproduce any time of day or night. Yet now, when it was real dawn outside and in, up there it would be everlasting black night until whatever god magicked it otherwise. Those little washed-out figures having a good long hibernation in their beds; the crouching watcher in the woods, the silent army pressed against the rocks; the defenders in the castle ... *I wish I'd seen them*, he thought; *there must have been more than that little tootling band and the one playing the trumpet. And I bet they'd be worth seeing, too.* The trumpeter had been kitted out in something that flashed in the sun, with a something else sharply colorful over the top of it. Morris could picture the rest of them like a brave band of knights, with swords and bows and arrows and pots of boiling oil. Out-of-this-world better than any fantasy game he'd ever seen.

However hard he squeezed his mind he could not remember what weapons, if any, the attackers had carried. And it was all just up there, above his head. They were separated by nothing more than a ceiling, a space, and a floor.

18   It must, he reflected after a blank few minutes, be

a very strong ceiling and floor, or all that vast setup must be very much lighter than it looks. The tree, the little conifer, was real; the grass had roots; that castle is *huge* and solid looking (*though I haven't touched it, be fair*). *Pianos are heavy. I've seen a piano upstairs in a house. The castle is bigger than a piano. Suppose it fell through the floor onto this bed.* But no, however otherworldly Patrick seemed, he was no fool. As *she* had said, in other words. And he's gone off to work, and the door to all that will be locked, and we're not going to stay here.

When this line of thinking became unbearable, Morris got out of bed, because he couldn't think about anything else. He drew back the skimpy curtains and gazed at the bleak December scene. It had gathered no great beauty since yesterday; in fact, it had no beauty at all. Even Morris, no country-lover, could appreciate why Patrick had given so much care to every detail of his private landscape upstairs. Whoever had built this house here must have hated other people: no one would choose to visit and stay in such a dreary spot.

Morris heard his mother moving about, clomping downstairs. Much as he disliked the idea, he knew he'd better get dressed and join her. He wondered and bet against himself which face she'd show today: the wound-up aggressive or the coldly silent. Sometimes it was the sadly hurt, but that was rare these days now Mr. Nelson was never around. On the whole, seeing she'd been cut off in mid-spate by Patrick's flight, Morris thought it would be the wound-up aggressive.

She was just closing a telephone conversation with the words, "Oh, thanks, Bea, I can't tell you how grateful I am—are you really sure? Oh yes, yes; thanks. Till then."

Seeing Morris, she knew he'd heard and understood. With a brief moment's compassion they both turned away, with no reproach on the one side or victory on the other. *Please don't gloat*, he prayed, and she didn't.

"Tea or coffee?" she asked, just like the olden days.

"Whatever you're making."

He wrenched open the kitchen outside door and stepped out into the paved yard. Looking up at the house he noticed a security alarm high on the wall; an unpainted box probably concocted by Patrick himself. The idea of any burglars staggering off with armfuls of castle country was quite funny.

Where, he wondered, were the blocked-up windows? When he found them, around another side of the house, he realized that they were not above his room. The only boarded windows on the top floor had yet another boarded window beneath. The laughter that had hurt him so had not come from that quarter at all.

"Morris, I'm going over to Della's."

"Again? What for?"

"Your coffee's in the kitchen. What are you doing out here? it's freezing." Mrs. Nelson glanced up at the house, scanning the blind windows. She could work it out for herself.

"Morris—"

"All right, I'm going."

"Don't—" Another glance at the windows.

He smiled falsely. "You don't have to tell me."

She rattled the car keys. He thought she would begin saying a lot of harsh things if he didn't do as she wanted, so he trundled back to the kitchen, to release her.

In daylight the house was possibly worse than at night. Everything was so visible, sordid and careless. With all that magnificence tucked away up two flights of stairs and behind three locked doors. Although Morris knew it to be useless, he drifted along with temptation, even simply to stand barred outside the room imagining the marvels within.

Taped to the door was a piece of paper:

MORRIS. Ring me at 205-4119 ext. 14.

Patrick

He turned it over several times as if expecting other words to appear by magic to explain the message. The door was locked—yes, so it was. This is a warning notice. *Of course, now that I've ripped it off the door he'll know I've been up here nosing around whether I ring him or not.* Morris tried stupidly to retape the paper into place. But what was to be lost by obeying the order? They were leaving the place too soon in any case. *If he bites my head off, so what, I'll never need to see him again.*

Even so, he stood a long time by the telephone, staring at the paper, working on a few defensive sentences, before he dialed the number. Nor did it help that Patrick had to be fetched ("Who's calling?"), which involved a waiting silence.

At last: "Hello? Morris?"

"Yes."

"You found my note."

"Yes—I—" The defensive sentences evaporated.

"Good." (*What?*) "First you must promise not to touch anything. And don't take that lightly, because I'd know, without doubt."

Morris found he couldn't breathe properly. This opening was not expected.

"Morris?" Patrick said, "are you still there?"

"Yes." He couldn't speak properly either.

"Right; do I hear you promise that? *No touching.*"

"Yes."

"You can look all you like—the light'll come on, as you know, and it'll have to suffice, till I'm home. You can't operate the console anyway, you don't know the key. The key to the *room* is in my bedroom—know where? Top left-hand drawer. Not usually, just today, in your honor. Got that?"

"Yes—you must think—yesterday, it was unlocked, you know, I didn't force it or anything."

"I know; my error; no, I didn't mean that, no harm. All right, Morris? I should be back by four-thirty today. What's your mother doing?"

"She's gone over to Aunt Della's again. You know

we're going—"

"So I believe. I'll see you then—and remember, no touching."

"Yes. Oh, thanks, thanks—"

The line was already dead.

| | | | | | | | | | | |

The lighting was not as it had been yesterday, but there was nothing he could do about it. The whole landscape was resting as in a slow, sunless evening. All Morris could hope was that it didn't progress into night. The castle was in deep shadow.

He saw that the setup was changed slightly. There were no figures around the base of the castle and, as far as he could make out, no lone watcher in the wood. He tried to see inside the farmhouse dormitory, but it wasn't possible. He walked very slowly down the complete length of the outer perimeter, which he hadn't done last night. It seemed that the trees thickened before ending quite suddenly, on higher ground again, a rough moorland with what looked incredibly like a real miniature lake and a wild stream flowing down into the farm pastures, under a packbridge, and into a village pond.

The water looked as real as everything else. Morris lay down on the ground as near the pond as possible, tempted by the idea that Patrick wouldn't know if he just dipped one finger into the water. Then he blinked and cursed the poor light: sheltering in the lee of the packbridge were three model figures, two with their backs toward him and the third facing in his direction. His eyes were on a level with their heads; they were, had he dared, within touching distance.

The figure turned toward him had a finely modeled face, shrouded with a hood or long hair. It was dressed in loose full-length garments; male or female, he couldn't tell. The whole was painted in the same camouflage as all the other outlanders he had seen. They were very hard to spot as they appeared to change color to any background, with skin coloring to match their clothing. It was almost unbearable, not to be able to touch, to bring the little figure just that fraction nearer. Of its own accord, one finger stretched out gently toward the model. All thought and reason had gone. But then.

The shrouded figure was watching him.

Not possible.

Even so. The eyes, that same non-color, were as still as ever. But the whites showed where no white had been. For a long moment, Morris and the tiny game piece exchanged unfrozen, intelligent glances; then the eyelids closed, tortoiselike, and the glance was veiled. Life gone quite away.

Morris shut his own eyes, viewing over and over again in the dark of his mind that open, human glance and its veiling. He couldn't bear to look again and see that he was wrong. *I'm not a kid*, he told himself, *but somehow I've been conned into acting like one*. The twilight in which he lay was persuading him that he was tired. He fell into a doze.

When he awoke, after maybe a few minutes, he saw that his hand was still resting loosely round the little figure. His fingers were loosely curved round its base of firmly planted feet. As he carefully withdrew his hand he thought that he must have been really holding it after all, for the plastic it was made from was almost as warm as his own skin.

He got up, and left the room.

4

He tried watching television, poking round the house, and scanning magazines (since he couldn't read them). Nothing induced the slightest interest. He vandalized an unopened box of cookies and tried some whiskey. Finally, expecting his mother's return at any time, he went out for a walk. There was only the one way to go, as far as the main road. A signpost pointed to his mother's old home ground, so he set face about and walked quickly in the opposite direction. The road was winding but with no great promise. Two girls on ponies passed by with haughty looks. A few houses were set back from the road. One of them boasted two fir trees in the front garden draped with colored lights. Morris had forgotten it was nearly Christmas. At the moment he had forgotten everything except that slow, penetrating stare from the tiny model figure, and the secret lowering of its eyelids. It had a hidden meaning, unfathomable, unless his mind was breaking down.

He grew tired of the road. As there was nowhere else to go, he turned round and walked back again. The weather, like the landscape, was featureless.

It was almost a relief to see his mother in the kitchen.

"Where've you been?" she asked.

"Out."

She glanced at his feet but he'd been wise enough to wear boots.

"Where to?"

"Just along and back."

"Now you've seen what it's like out here," she said. "But he would stay on."

"Patrick? What do you mean?"

"This used to be our grandfather's brother's house. Patrick always hung round him—the old man was just like him; he left it to him in his will. . . ." Morris saw that she was switched on again, not really talking to him. Here's another old wound being aired. "The old man's wife didn't count, or his daughter, our Aunt Josie; oh no, let her find somewhere else to live; Patrick's the one, all boys together. . . ." She surfaced from her bitter monologue. "What're you staring at, Morris?" she asked in surprise. "You men are all the same."

"But," Morris argued, "you said yourself what a dreary hole this is and who'd want to live here, so why shouldn't Patrick have it if he wants?"

His mother glared. "That is quite beside the point," she said coldly.

"*And* you must have known what staying here was going to be like, for us," Morris went on, scenting victory. "However long ago it was you last came

27

here, it can't have been that different, all these rooms and that outside can't have changed since the Stone Age."

She sniffed, offended. "Many years ago," she said carefully, "when there were women making the best of this house, it was at least comfortable, with real furniture you could feel at home with and proper use made of this kitchen. When I was a child . . ."

"I bet it's the same furniture here now," Morris grinned.

"Very likely." She straightened her back, undefeated. "Anyway, we'll be on our way first thing tomorrow and then I don't want to hear another word about it."

The secret glance printed into his mind again. It stopped him arguing any further. It was something in which his mother had no remote part.

Because she was there, he also couldn't go back into that place to see if everything there was still the same as when he'd left. He was sure she was keeping a practiced eye on him. Go up there and she'd be stealing after him, discovering and scorning all the marvels. He thought of the key, safely back in Patrick's room, burning a hole in his mind; he thought of the one last evening in this house (probably shared with lucky Ian); he thought more than any other thing of the little shrouded figure . . . and there thought ended.

It was hard, at Patrick's return, not to jump up like a crazy oversized puppy and start to pester him for

favors. Patrick listened quite patiently to his sister's long tale of her day's proceedings and plans for tomorrow. He said, at last, "You do what you please, Annie, it's all one."

"I've been grateful, of course; I know you're not used to visitors." A great concession; she could afford to be generous now she didn't have to stay.

Patrick said, "Oh, you'll find living alone has its compensations."

Morris drew a quick breath. She didn't care for that remark.

"You," she told her brother, "don't have offspring to bring up. At least, I hope you don't."

Patrick laughed, almost "ha ha!" and looked at Morris. "Could you imagine," he said. "And what about you, Morris? What are you going to do tomorrow?"

"Is there a choice?" Morris muttered.

"Better ask your mother."

Far from it; he didn't even dare risk a hopeful glance.

She said, "You don't know you're born, Patrick; you haven't a clue."

"Quite right," he agreed. "Well, Morris, how about an hour or two, if your mother'll let you come out to play?"

Morris winced, disliking Patrick just then. How easy it was for him.

As they went upstairs Patrick asked for the key.

"I put it back," Morris said stiffly. "I was only in there a short while."

"Oh? Don't you like it then?"

"I was only looking."

29

Patrick retrieved the key, but stood weighing it

from hand to hand. "Morris," he said, "put your claws in. Let *them*—" he pointed upstairs—"do the fighting while you watch. It's never worth it."

Inside the vast room, he set a switch, then asked Morris to close the door. The lights stayed on, the door quietly locked itself.

"Now Morris, I need your help. Come down here and I'll show you. What are you looking at? What's wrong?"

"I promise you I didn't touch them," Morris said.

"What?"

"These three figures. They've moved since I was here. I didn't touch them." (No, but it had been close.)

With stronger light on the scene, Patrick knelt beside Morris.

"I don't know what the little buggers are doing there anyway," he murmured. "They've no right, but they've done it before."

"Done what?"

"Wandered about between games."

Morris unscrambled his mind enough to think, *either he's crazy or I am.* "How can they?" he asked.

"God only knows. I've already written a strong letter of complaint to the firm, but they'll only disclaim. Typical. Now, how have they moved?"

"They were right against that bridge and now they're up the bank nearly on the road. And you see how they've all got their backs to us—but before, one of them was facing this way." He found he couldn't say, was facing *me*. In an odd way he felt he was betraying them. Very well. How dare that haunting face be turned away!

As Patrick returned to the console to view the figures in close-up on the screen, Morris asked, "Why can't we touch them?"

"Oh, we can, but it's not really advisable, and if they'd behave themselves, it shouldn't be necessary. Got them. Back view; left side; front. Come and see. Which is the culprit?"

Morris would have said, how should I know, supposing the model figures to have been churned out by the identical thousand in a factory. Now, close to the screen, he could see three similar yet differing faces, two male, one female; the male faces lined and stern (one almost angry), the female face young and pensive. Her long hair was parted in the middle and over it she wore a loose hooded cloak. The modeling was finely detailed even to a wisp of hair across her forehead.

"That's her," Morris said. *Oh, traitor.*

"Butter wouldn't melt," Patrick murmured. "Good aren't they? Real quality. So they ought to be, what they cost."

Morris nodded, transfixed, waiting to see her lift her eyes and praying that she wouldn't. "Have they got names?" he asked.

Patrick was amused. "No, but they're all numbered. So when they get absorbed they're replaced, each one. It's very clever."

"How do you mean, absorbed?"

"By the castle."

"How?"

"It eats them."

"Always? All of them?"

31

"So far. There's a master strategy, but they haven't worked it out yet."

"*They* haven't? The model figures?"

"Well—" Patrick grinned foolishly, as if caught out—"the computer. That is to say, it will have of course, but it plays along with the lesser brains." He tapped his head. "Until then, glop glop glop and in they all go."

Morris felt unsettled. "And what happens to them?"

"Ah. It doesn't let on. Mincemeat, I expect. Then they're replaced, reincarnated, resurrected."

"The same characters?"

"Goodness knows. Who cares, as long as they keep on coming."

Morris stared at the frozen faces on the screen; at that one frozen face. "How long do they last be-fore—"

"Not so long," Patrick admitted. "It depends mostly on how often we play and the tactics. Some come out first time and get swallowed up just—" He gulped. "I daresay others last longer. I don't follow individual fortunes, though it's an idea; could give a new slant I suppose. I'll see what Ian thinks." He reached out and the screen went blank. Morris held the afterimage of that face for a few seconds, then it too died.

He pulled himself together. "What will you do about those three?" he asked. "Will you move them?"

Patrick shrugged. "Include them in a program, why not; we can do that. If they want to shift, let's shift them." He began to consult his file, scanning previous and possible assaults. Morris would have gone back to stay close to the three, but Patrick said, "Now's your big moment; these are the lighting controls; see number 3? Lower it slowly—that'll do—now number 4 up a bit. Behold, winter moonlight."

And so it was, cold, clear, casting long blue shadows; all it needed to complete the illusion was a covering of snow.

"And now," Patrick announced, "my latest trick!" He turned from the console, swept his arms wide, and lo, the sleeping landscape was covered with the thin, glinting whiteness of first snow.

They stood and admired. "I've only just added this," Patrick confided. "You're the first to see."

"It's tremendous," Morris said.

"I can do thunder and lightning too, but no rain."

When Morris returned to his three troublemakers he saw that they too were lightly iced with white.

"Right," Patrick said. "Winter sound effects, enter conspirators."

A wolf howled in the forest and was answered. Like shadows, the three figures were joined by nine more. They huddled together as if discussing tactics.

As they began to move in single file along the road toward the castle, Patrick said, "I've set it to run by itself now."

"Do you know what they they'll do?" asked Morris.

"Fifty-fifty."

"But can you change what happens halfway through, if you want?"

No answer. "Look," Patrick said gleefully, "they've left the road for the south castle wall."

How are they powered? Morris wondered. In ab-

33

solute silence, the dozen figures separated into pairs to investigate the ground close by the castle wall. Their movements were marvelously lifelike.

"Which one's your culprit?" Patrick asked.

Morris had to admit he didn't know.

The figures re-formed into three groups of four, busily doing something to the ground.

"Sappers," Patrick explained, "mining under the wall. They've tried it before but it didn't work. Now keep an eye on the—wait a minute!"

A stray figure appeared from the forest and started making frantic, silent gestures to the furthest group. Patrick rushed to illuminate the screen, cursing his choice of moonlight. The little group, pulled by their friend into the shelter of the castle wall, was completely camouflaged.

"Where did he spring from?" Patrick cried.

"Warning them," Morris murmured.

"Not in *my* plot. Aha—"

Sudden arrows whistled from slits in the wall. The sound effects of bodies in mortal pain were chilling. The unwounded fled, attacked by more deadly arrows. Only two escaped. The far group, unnoticed, melted into the trees behind the castle with their rescuer. There were no heroics, no saving of wounded comrades. After a pause, a small door opened. Two figures hauling a kind of barrow emerged, with an escort of two armed men. While the bodies were being piled onto the barrow the armed men stood watch. Morris thought he heard at least one of the
34 supposed corpses cry out in despair or terror. Any

one of them could be *her*, and he'd never know. The barrow was escorted back into the castle and the door closed, leaving the scene once more a pretty winter picture.

"That'll teach them to wander about without leave," said Patrick.

"It wasn't very—military," Morris remarked.

"Most sieges aren't. Let's see—" Patrick adjusted the viewer to scan the snow-covered site of the incident, then zoomed in rapidly. "You see," he pointed out, "they were already into the ground. They tried it before; they learn by experience. All that has to be taken into account for future bouts. It's good, isn't it." And he actually rubbed his hands.

Morris said, "What happens now?"

"Shut it down, log the details."

"Those others, that escaped—"

"Shut them down too." And he did so.

After the long moment's complete darkness, separate lighting at the console let Patrick attend to his report. "Shut the door after you, please, Morris," he said absently.

| | | | | | | | | | | |

Where is she—swallowed by the castle? Hiding in the forest? I'll never know.

It pursued him through the night, the real, long night.

But their night is longer than ours and could last forever if Patrick gets tired of the game.

They don't know that, of course. They don't really know 35 *anything. Just because they're such clever models and the game's so sophisticated, you can be fooled into thinking them real people.*

I can be fooled. Patrick isn't, and he knows better. Though—

In and out of unquiet sleep, Morris worried each statement through. Always, that face hung behind his mind, as disturbing as a giant image wavering in the sky. Sometimes she looked at him, sometimes the mouth moved; but no sound ever came.

5

At 7:45 a.m. Patrick shambled into the kitchen for his usual early mug of tea. Because he wasn't really awake, he couldn't understand why Morris was there, asleep, with his head on the table. Respecting another being's need for rest, he put the kettle on quietly, and when Morris woke suddenly, apologized for the disturbance and poured milk into a second mug.

Morris said, "I had to see you before you went to work. Because we're going today."

Patrick looked as if he'd forgotten that. "But you don't have to if you don't want," he said.

"It's what Mum wants."

Patrick nodded. "Well, thanks, but you didn't have to wait up."

"No, it's about the room."

"What room? You mean the castle setup? Oh yes?"

"I wondered, can I go in and have a last look? I won't touch anything."

"Why not? Did you sleep down here just for that? I thought after last evening you didn't care for the game." 37

Morris accepted tea gratefully. "I do really," he said.

"You wanted a proper fight though, didn't you; knights-in-armor and drums and trumpets and stirring deeds."

"The trumpet was good," Morris admitted.

"But that was the day before. You had to miss it, yes." Patrick glanced at his watch. "Can't do it now," he said, "sorry. Here, you can have an inspection, but mind the rules." The precious key was transferred from an inner pocket to Morris's hand. "Put it in the drawer after. Oh, and if you go before I'm back, wish Annie a Merry Christmas from me. She likes little niceties, doesn't she?"

"I don't want to go," Morris said.

Patrick was in a hurry now. "Look," he said, "I told you, you're welcome to stay, with or without your mother, but sorry, I'm not going to get in a family row about it—don't you know what they're like once they're switched on? You sort it out, Morris, and let me know, all right?"

It was probable he'd heard the footsteps coming down stairs, the speed with which he vanished. Seconds later, Mrs. Nelson was asking Morris, "Has Patrick gone?" and then, seeing that he had, "You're up early, aren't you?"

"We were talking."

"Oh dear."

He concealed the key, his talisman. He decided to give calm reasoning a try. "Mum," he began. "I get on with Patrick very well."

"He's your uncle," she reminded him.

Unsure of the meaning of that, Morris ventured a quick nod. "He said I'm welcome to stay on here. He said it several times." She sighed deeply. "If you tell me *why* I can't stay, we could talk round it a bit."

The phrase was not well chosen. "No thanks, Morris," his mother said, "I've had enough talking round things lately to last a lifetime. This isn't a sensible place for you to stay alone, and that's that, playing silly games all the time—"

He abandoned reason. "You're old-fashioned and narrow-minded!"

"Right."

"You never think of *me*, only what other people'll say about *you*—and I bet they never say anything, they couldn't care less!"

"I do what's best for you."

"Treating me like a baby, dragging me around—other boys of sixteen—"

"Grow up, Morris, and I'll treat you like it."

They'd said it all before; the accusations had lost nearly all bite and meaning. Only now she brought him up sharply by asking suddenly, "What's so attractive here, anyway?"

"I get on with—Patrick."

"Playing games!"

"Don't sneer." (*Oh, be guarded.*) "He's very clever. He could teach me a lot—more—than at school."

She turned away with a brush of the hand. "Oh, give it up, Morris. I wish I'd never brought you here. My fault, I admit it; now I'm putting it right. Finish." **39**

He had been on the point of offering her a sight of the room's wonders as a last forlorn hope, but felt such a surge of bitter hatred against her blindness that the plea could not be made.

She said, "Bea's expecting us about midday. Go away and play, Morris—oh, don't alarm yourself, I won't spy on you—and be ready and civilized when I want you."

He knew, oddly enough, that he could trust her word.

The light that came on at the door's opening was the standard steady sunrise. Morris shut the door; the light faded and came back. His first thought was, *Patrick forgot to cancel the last weather*; then he cried aloud, "Hey!" for the snow that had been a light dusting was now as deep as a long night's layering. It was a great temptation, but he stopped himself from dipping a finger to test its reality. As the light grew stronger the ground was washed with pink. Wondering how the deep snowfall was contrived, Morris even glanced up at the ceiling, but saw no magic sprinklers.

It was wonderful. He thought he'd be cunning and look for telltale footprints, but found none. They were either more cunning than he, or truly and simply as shut down as they ought to be. He went to examine the scene of last night's scuffle, but of course it was wiped out. " 'Deep and crisp and even,' " Morris hummed to himself, past the north side of the castle and along the boundary of the forest. " 'Brightly shone the moon that night . . .' " He grinned, despite himself. " 'When a poor man came in sight, gathering winter fu-well.' "

He got down on the floor again to peer between the trees, quite expecting to see the poor old man beneath his load of sticks.

No. Of course not. Though the woodland view was like the memory of a mythical childhood. That little group that had escaped into the forest, where were they now?

As Morris regretfully stood up, something glinted and flashed in the sunlight. A solitary lookout stood at gaze on a castle turret; a tiny man in polished armor and a crimson cloak. Glorious, but too far away. Morris anguished over the blank monitor screen that he couldn't warm to life.

He wandered the length of the forest until he could look back at the castle as from far away. Warped by some strange perspective, the fortress shimmered with the mystical beauty of a timeless saga. These poor drab peasants, Morris related to himself, are driven by hereditary compulsion to spend their entire lives trying to take the castle. It was easy to plot the story; not so easy to be sure which side to be on, whom to relate to.

He lay down at the very foot of the landscape, to see the quest at their eye level. For perhaps two seconds he knew such a terror of yearning that he felt his heart would shatter.

She was there, standing in the shadow of a barn. The wall was flecked stone and so was she, but her eyes were steadily watching him and her mouth com- 41 pressed with fierce self-control, being so closely observed.

He whispered, "You *are* the same one, aren't you? You escaped."

She made no sign.

"Do you hear me?" he went on, a little louder. "You can move now if you want to; I won't do anything. I'm only watching."

He thought her glance shifted very slightly.

"I wouldn't harm you," he said. "Please move from there if you want to. Trust me."

Her head turned slowly, to see him better. The movement was quite natural. Then she shut her eyes.

"Are you programmed to speak?" Morris asked. For his sanity's sake it was best to remember that she was only a drab piece in a huge game.

A faint sound, between a buzz and a hum, entered his head. He concentrated hard. Silence, then the sound again, intermittent and slightly varying in pitch. He said quietly, "If you want to speak you'll have to make it louder, or slower; I'm not used to it yet." He waited. When the sound came again he watched her face closely. Her mouth was surely moving.

Because of Patrick's warning, he didn't dare reach out to bring her nearer. Instead, he wriggled as close as he could without destroying any scenery. She opened her eyes once and immediately shut them again. *I'm a terrible size*, Morris told himself, and stopped trying to get any nearer.

42   "Speak now," he murmured.

After a taut silence, he distinctly heard the words, "Are you our God?"

"Oh no."

More sounds he couldn't translate, ending, "Be merciful."

It seemed she didn't believe him. He said, "You escaped."

"Even so." For the first time, she moved her hands out of the folds of her hooded cloak; a gesture of ritual thanks.

He said, "I didn't do it for you. Someone warned you."

... something, something ... "Deserve it. Next time ... better."

"Next time, no," Morris said. "Stay away from there."

She looked up in surprise. "We vowed it, Lord." The words quite clear; brave and foolish.

"But they'll get you."

"Yes."

"I don't want them to."

She frowned, not comprehending, then she smiled. The hands repeated their simple gesture.

He said, "Do you know what happens to your people, in the castle?"

"We fear and hope." Her gaze defied him to tell her otherwise, so he kindly said nothing. Besides, the role of lesser god, even if denied, wouldn't allow him to admit ignorance.

"Do you have a name?" he asked.

"Farmhouse."

"No; your name, not where you live."

"Just so. My kin and home, all Farmhouse."

"Well," Morris decided, "I'll find you a better name."

She said, "Our kin is the best, Lord." Such a brave little thing.

Morris, a stern voice ground in his head, *that brave little thing is no more than a programmed component in a game. You've been talking to a* toy. *Yet she—it—answers rationally. How could a computer have put in ready answers to what I didn't know I was going to say? Unless I've imagined the whole thing. Try to catch it out.*

"How many kin have you?" he asked suddenly.

"Five."

"Still five? After last night?"

"Our God will renew."

"How many kin have you *now?*"

"One."

So God's renewal must wait on Patrick (the Greater God?) starting a new game. "And what are you doing out here?" Morris asked.

"Waiting." And she seemed to freeze, to remember her role.

The stern inner voice pointed out to Morris what a dummy he was. He stood up and rubbed his eyes. She was a cleverly contrived little model figure, nothing more. *I'm going nuts*, he thought.

He replaced the key, went downstairs, and was qui-
44 etly obedient to his mother's every wish. She was sur-

prised, suspicious but grateful, having pictured sporadic fighting between them for the rest of the day at least. Yet his docility made her uncomfortable: somewhere she'd heard how too much stress can tip a person's mind into a sleepwalking state. It frightened her. Poor Morris—too old to be protected, too young to be independent. Could she leave him here, maybe? No, surely Bea's sane household must be better.

She tried to be nice to him, pointing out old and well-loved places as they neared the house: "Do you remember, Morris . . ." and silly little tales of her own childhood. He wished she would leave him alone, seeing her jollity as a sign of victory. She felt him edge away and, baffled, gave it up.

As they arrived, he was aware that Cousin Bea's house was very different from Patrick's. There was going to be no private space for him. A tiny room of his own, but that was all. At least Bea didn't have a son with whom he'd have to share, only a little girl. He steeled his heart against the little girl. They were being nice to him all over again, smiling and encouraging and ignoring his stolid silence. Then his mother drew Bea away with false delight, seeing what a waste of time it was. He sat on the bed and stared at a whimsical picture on the opposite wall, so close he could almost swipe at it. He looked out of the small window, surprised that the house was on an unnoticed hill; that beyond the houses across the road there were trees and hedged fields. *I shall go out there*, he promised himself. *I won't stay cooped up in here.* 45

It wasn't right. Whenever, wherever his gaze fixed for longer than a couple of seconds, the real view became overlaid with scenes from the castle landscape and the sparse events he'd witnessed there. Little figures trekked in the moonlight to mine the walls; they were attacked and cruelly died and were carted away. Little figures hid and fled into the trees, and one of them later stood and talked with him. He saw these things over and over again through the day as he ate, sat, supposedly watched TV, with other people who only rarely took on more substance than the ones he'd rather see. There was the lookout on the tower as well. The castle figures were brightly dressed and armed, and he'd hardly had a chance to glance at them yet.

The curtains were drawn, the lights on, various strangers were milling around. Somebody bounced up to him and shouted in his ear. It was Bea's little girl, whose name he didn't remember.

"The telephone!" she bawled. "There's someone for you!"

"I'm not deaf," he said.

"Well you act like it. It's in the hall." And she bounded away.

It was Patrick. He gave Morris no time to wonder what he'd done. "Look," he said, "did you go up there? You must have done, what about all that snow? What did you do?"

"Nothing. It was like that, as if it'd been snowing
46 all night."

In the silence, Morris gripped the receiver willing Patrick to believe him. "Morris," he said, "if I thought you'd tampered—"

"No, no! I swear it! It was like that!"

"And what else?"

"What else? I don't know what you mean."

"Villagers out on the green—the white now—having a meeting."

"I didn't put them there, I wouldn't know how," Morris protested.

"Well, I'm damn sure *I* didn't," Patrick said. "Were they there when you had a look?"

"Only one."

"Well, there's six seven eight now, all with their heads together plotting mischief. That blasted computer, I'll—well, thanks, Morris, keep in touch."

"Don't go!" Morris cried. "Look, can't I come over?"

"Well, of course; can you get here?"

"Oh wait, I'll go and see, hang on!" Morris burst into the domestic scene with a plea for a lift to East Lodge. His mother gazed at him, completely baffled. It was a waste of time. He went back and said to Patrick, "Sorry, I can't just now. Some other time?"

"Surely. No stupid computer's going to beat me. See you, Morris."

He couldn't face going back into that cozy room. He should have known better than to make a fool of himself.

The little girl was sitting by herself, in semi-darkness on the stairs.

"Did you enjoy that?" Morris asked coldly. "Excuse me."

She drew herself aside to let him by.

"Spies hear things they don't like, in the end," Morris told her.

She tipped back her head to look at him upside down. Either she was pulling a silly face or that was her natural expression. With amazing speed she pursued Morris to his room before he could shut the door.

"Get out," he said.

"I live here," she stated.

"I know that. This is my room, while I'm here."

"That picture's mine."

"You can have it; it's horrible." He reached up, unhooked the picture, and gave it to her. "Now get out."

She glared at him. "I don't want you here."

"That makes two of us. Bloody women."

The eyes widened. "I'm telling."

"You do that. Go on." He pushed the door against her bulk.

"When my sister Claire and my dad come back, I'm telling. They're bigger than you."

"I'm terrified." He shoved again. She yelled as the door trapped her hand, and withdrew backward. Morris leaned against the shut door, which had no lock.

48 "And stay out!" he shouted.

He lay on the bed awaiting judgment. When none came, his mind began to relax and admit once again images of that other marvelous place; and that face, always that steady, hooded face.

It went with him into sleep.

6

Christmas was suddenly unavoidable. The house was completely turned over to it. Morris made the mistake of entering a room where the little girl and a similar friend were making paper decorations. "Look," said the little girl to her scandalized friend, "*he* squashed my hand in the door."

"Really? Oh, Kelly, it's all colors."

"I know," turning the hand around to catch the light and Morris's eye. "But I didn't tell."

"Oh, Kelly."

Morris left, followed by giggles. He informed the mince-pie makers that he was going into town. They were far too busy to bother. It wasn't much of a town; once on the old stagecoach routes, now surrounded by neat estates yet still rural. Surely, Morris reasoned, it must be possible to get fairly near to East Lodge by public transport.

In the end, the only hope was a train which stopped at a small village some distance away, but no return train in the evening. He quickly bought several identical boxes of chocolates as presents, and went back to the house. The chocolates, displayed, might soften his mother's heart, especially as she looked so kitchen-flushed and happy helping Cousin Bea with the cooking. It was like a very old memory that made Morris want to cry. Unfortunately, that wouldn't do.

He announced, "I've found a train, so can I go to Patrick's this evening?" *And please don't shout at me,* his mind begged.

"Oh, Morris." She rubbed her cheek, almost as though he'd hit her.

"Mum, please; I must."

"Must? What is this? How will you get back?"

"Maybe Patrick'll bring me, or you could."

"Oh yes? Can you see Patrick doing that? Putting himself out for anybody? Can you?"

"I suppose not. I'm sorry—as soon as I can take driving lessons—"

"Roll on the day." (False wish.) "So it's up to soft old mother again."

Morris put in quickly, "Or I could stay there overnight. He said I could, anytime."

"You can forget that. You know, Morris, I'd really thought you were past playing with toys."

He wouldn't rise to the bait.

So she said, "If I do this, it'll be for this once and no more. Do you hear me?" She waited. "Do you hear me?"

"Yes, Mum."

"And not late, and no moans when I turn up there."

He nodded. "Thanks, Mum."   51

"I don't know what Bea'll say."

A little while later, Morris, behind the door, heard Bea say, "You're a fool, Annie, I tell you, I'd never let either of my two go over there without me—grown men playing with toys, what an example!"

"Who's spying now?" Kelly suddenly asked at his elbow.

| | | | | | | | | | | |

Patrick was surprised to see Morris but welcoming. "Old Ian'll be here soon," he said, "then we can get our heads together." And as they trailed upstairs he continued to complain about the faulty computer in technical terms that might as well have been Ancient Russian to Morris. He thought, *Patrick doesn't have a clue how I feel about this.*

"There," Patrick said, "you see? I ordered all that blasted snow away, watched it disappear, left it, and what do I find? It's all back again. Some malfunction —and it's not the cheapo range, you know." He paced up and down, working up to a fine wrath. "You know how much this little lot cost me? No, and I don't like to think of it either. Top quality merchandise? Freak weather, models running amok; they'll be running their own campaigns next. I might as well be sitting watching somebody else's bloody video. I won't have it, you hear, *I won't have it!*"

Don't ever cross Patrick, his knowing mother had advised Morris. Now he could see why. Pressed against the wall, he watched Patrick rage. He ventured to say, "But, Patrick, it's still marvelous."

52   "Marvelous? It's bloody useless!" And Patrick

aimed a loose kick at a little cottage behind the home farm, gashing a great hole in its wall and roof.

Without stopping to look, he moved on, muttering and cursing. "And where are the rebs now?" he demanded. "All tucked up in their little beds, no doubt. Well, we'll see, we'll flush them out!" He strode to the console, illuminated the screen and jerkily homed in on the sleeping farmhouse.

Gently, Morris knelt by the wrecked cottage. Tiny stones and tiles were tumbled into the snow, several very close to him. With one eye on Patrick he extended a finger and trickled one of the stones into his hand. Surely not plastic. And snow, melting on the tip of his finger. Impossible. Morris tipped the stone back into place and lowered his head to see through the gaping hole in the wall.

He drew breath. Two little people stood inside, staring out. If they were shell-shocked, they didn't show it, nor did they flinch at the gigantic eye looming at them. Little dust-colored models; how could they?

Patrick ordered Morris to get his head out of the way. He looked up to see the ruined wall appear on the monitor, then the two figures, out of focus, then sharp. They were two males, bearded, stolid, almost Biblical, staring back at the unseen camera without a blink. Now Patrick dabbed at a keyboard, still muttering. The two bearded figures stayed frozen on the screen.

As from another world, the front doorbell rang. Amazingly, Patrick said to Morris, "Look, this is the monitor control panel—quick, man—have a look for   53 yourself, I'll be back directly." Outside the door, he shouted, "And don't touch anything else!"

Carefully, carefully, Morris withdrew from the sorry cottage, thinking, *There, now you can breathe again*, to the little men. He wasn't very adept at focusing on anywhere else. Here was a stretch of snowy ground, another building, a shut door, a window.

A voice said, "How're you doing?" Ian was peering over his shoulder. "Just a minute." He adjusted the picture so that they could view into the room. "A blank. Let's try another." Beneath his expert hand the scene slid gently by. "What exactly are we looking for?" he asked.

"There was one particular figure that seemed to be able to move around," Morris said, then added "ha-ha" to show how silly that was.

But Ian nodded. Patrick said, "Come on, then, let's find it."

They intruded impartially into each building, some empty, some not. Those in the farmhouse were asleep in their beds, as before.

"We can rouse them out, if you want," Ian said. "A simple little flip, no more."

"No thanks," Morris said. "Carry on."

Another building, another room, four figures sitting close around a fire.

"Hold it!"

"Yes? Right." Ian shouted to Patrick to come.

With sudden misgivings Morris asked, "What will he do?"

54   "Remove the offender, of course. Get the rogue component out, may well do the trick. Look," he

said to Patrick, "Morris has found it for us. Shall we go in?"

"Why not. Good old Morris. Which one is it again?"

"Second from the left," Morris the double traitor lied.

Ian adjusted the picture for a clearer view of the faces. They were all turned slightly away.

"Are you sure?" Patrick perhaps remembered better than he affected.

"Oh yes."

Patrick hesitated, either in thought or to give Morris a second chance. Then he delved about at the back of the room and came back with a long skinny metal gadget. Ian opened the door of the little building by remote control and Patrick inserted the end of the gadget among the figures. With great care, the supposed offender was lifted out and placed on the floor. Handing the gadget to Morris, Patrick picked up the tiny figure and displayed it on the palm of his hand. It was a man.

"This one?" Patrick asked.

Morris couldn't speak.

"I think," Patrick went on, "we'd best have all four out, just to be sure."

"What about the overall balance of numbers?" Ian wondered.

"Shouldn't affect it. Besides," Patrick reminded him, "these cowboy manufacturers owe me for faulty goods. Here Morris, hold this villain while I go back in." 55

"Suppose it isn't even one of those," Ian said.

"Then someone's going to lose a lifetime's pocket money."

"Or removing them won't cure the fault?"

"We shall see."

The little man lost all life as Morris held him. His three companions were brought out with equal care and set on the floor, where they too became color-drained and rigid. Morris knelt to place the first figure with them. They looked like expensive chess pieces without purpose; three male, one female.

She's dead, he thought. *I killed her.*

Patrick and Ian had lost interest in them already, discussing the best program to test out the purified setup. They set to work: first the snow melted or faded away within seconds. Then a quick tan-tara from inside the castle, and the band began to appear on the battlements.

It was grievous, to be able to touch her now she had no life, yet to be so stirred by the bright music that the dead must be abandoned.

"Patrick," Morris said, "what about these models?"

"Chuck them out, what you like." Patrick was happy now.

"Shouldn't you keep them for exchange at least?" Ian asked.

"Oh yes, quite right. Shove them in a box or something, Morris. Come and see this!"

He couldn't bear to look at their calcified faces as he carried and deposited them in the far corner. *Oh, I'm sorry*, he thought hard at her. *Oh, I'm sorry. Perhaps* 56 *later on I can—*

Patrick called him again, the trumpets sounded distant but clear across the countryside: To arms, to arms; a cheer went up from the castle, answered by another from without. Morris left the dead to see some real action at last, armor and weapons flashing in the sunlight, fierce glory and excitement.

Already a crowd of attackers was bringing up battering rams to the great doors; they carried burning torches high, to distract the castle archers. Smoke rose up and pierced Morris's nostrils and eyes; the attackers reached the doors, shouting, heaving, and thudding again and again. From the battlements above archers aimed and loosed at the orders of a fully armored knight, sword in one hand, fluttering pennon in the other.

On the monitor, the scene switched and zoomed with breathless speed. "Come on!" Morris shouted. "Come on! Heave! Heave!"

Now there were only enough men to carry one battering ram; they re-formed, with fire protectors (one, only a lad, plucked the torch from a shot comrade and held it on high: Morris's heart swelled with pride) for a last assault on the doors. With an almighty crash, the wood splintered, the bolts gave way. The brave lad jumped first through the gaping gash, the ram was dropped, the rest followed at a cheer.

"Quick!" Patrick urged Ian. "Inside view, they've breached!"

The scene on the monitor changed, a courtyard thick with smoke and out-of-focus fighting men.

"Where's the lad?" Morris cried. "Can't you find him?" It was only possible now to watch via the screen, with the action hidden by the castle walls.

Patrick started a countdown: "Ten, nine, eight . . ."

The fighting lasted for a count of four beyond zero. Then silence. Morris said, "What—"

"Great stuff," said Patrick. "I reckon we've got it beat."

"Is it over?"

"For this time. They'll repair the door and clear the dead, who'll be replaced, outside, all ready for the next round. And, this is the clever bit, the next lot'll *know* about that weakened door, which will affect the strategy, you see. *That's* the way, not all that subversive underground rubbish."

And I'd forgotten her so soon.

7

here is a cold, bleak time in the middle of the night when despair sits at the foot of the bed waiting to infect and smother the unsleeper. So Morris woke up and was at once confronted by his own treachery, grinning like an old friend and eager to play.

I couldn't help it, Morris opened.

Of course you could. You pointed her out to them.

I didn't know they'd take her away.

Kill, *not take away.*

She can't be killed, she was never alive.

Oh? She moved around by herself; she talked to you.

A programmed game piece.

You believed in her. You needed her. Because there's no one else. Is there? Now you've killed it.

That's stupid.

Yes? Who else will pay you a god's attention? Who else has any time for you at all? Go on then, name them.

I didn't want to be a god.

Oh, Morris, you make me laugh. You poor old thing; can't put two thoughts together these days, can you. All right, if she wasn't alive, you've only hurt 59 *yourself, and look what that could lead to. Victim of the Year, Morris Nelson.*

No. No. Leave me alone.

| | | | | | | | | | | |

Another morning, another day, and all they can talk about is Christmas; Christmas this and that as if it was so important.

"Hello," Kelly said to Morris. "I've been once to that funny house."

"What funny house?"

"Where you went last night, where you were before."

"Who says it's funny? I don't think so."

"He's funny." She tapped her forehead.

"You don't know anything about it."

"He plays stupid games. I've *seen*, so I do know."

It was humiliating even to consider that such a little birdbrain had ever shared Patrick's treasure. Yet Morris didn't doubt she spoke the truth. "And did your mommy stay and hold your hand?" he asked.

She laughed, highly delighted. Female minds were beyond him.

"Today," Mrs. Nelson informed him, "you're going to devote yourself to goodwill to all men."

"But not women," Morris muttered.

"Don't be funny."

That word funny again: funny house, funny farm . . .

"You owe it to me, Morris," his mother went on.

Oh, life was full of traps: if I do this you must do that, then it's turn about, always on the lookout to score another point against, always *against*. He reminded her, "I said thanks for fetching me from East Lodge last night. I really am grateful."

She said, "There was rather more to it than that. Bea thought I was mad to let you go there at all."

"All right," he said, swallowing retaliation, "I'll be good."

She looked at him with suspicion. "There's shopping to do. Here's a list, all supermarket stuff, easy. Here's the money. You can borrow Claire's bike to carry the goods."

"Claire?"

"Bea's elder girl."

"I'm not going on a kid's bike."

"She's as old as you. Now, Morris, I've a lot to do myself, so just get on with it." She handed him the list and money. "And when you come back, take the small trouble of letting Bea know, with a *courteous smile*."

And when I've done all that, he wondered, *will it be my turn for a favor?*

"But please," she said finally, "don't ask me to be a taxi service any more, because the answer is no." She knew him too well.

As the bicycle was not a perfect disgrace, he decided to utilize the courteous smile to ask Bea if he could use the bike for the rest of the day.

"I suppose so," she said, "though it's a pity your mother isn't here just now to say."

"Where is she?" Morris asked.

"Being busy." She cleared her throat. "She has a lot to do, you know," she said. "It's not easy for her."

"I know that."

"I don't think you do. All that trouble with your father—appalling, but I'm willing to bet she protected you from it."

Thinking of the useful bike, Morris said politely, "I have been there all the time; I really do know."

"She's very unhappy."

"Yes."

"He's been so vicious, so vindictive—and then to walk out like that."

"But that was best; it was murder, the two of them together."

Cousin Bea stared at Morris deeply. Instinct telling him she was about to delve into recent torment, he said quickly, "Can I go now?"

She smiled and even said, "I'm sorry."

| | | | | | | | | | | |

Since it seemed pointless to ride over to East Lodge, Morris simply went off into the nearest lanes; just to get away from the sound of female voices. One female voice traveled with him and was not to be dismissed. *Farmhouse; how could anyone be called Farmhouse? I would have called her* . . . no names came to mind. He got off the bike by a public footpath sign to see if the track was too muddy. It looked all right. The track was soon joined by a stream in parallel. On the left-hand side, an untrimmed hedge with gently sloping fields behind. Then a gate in the hedge and a path leading up to a real farmhouse, with several more buildings nearby. Morris stopped at the gate and gazed across at the farm. A dog ran barking from left to right, and a woman came to the doorway and called. From some hidden place an unknown animal bleated. The field between here and there was spiked with the tall skeletons of umbrella-ribbed plants. Just inside the gate was a handpainted notice:

VAIL FARM

Morris knew nothing about farms. If *she'd* lived, that name would have done very well. "Vail," he said aloud. "I name you Vail." Then he rode away, quite comfortable; solemn and self-warmed.

In December, it isn't so easy to keep cycling around without food and a purpose. Morris trundled back to the little town for chocolate and drink. As he came out of the shop he glanced casually at the cars parked in the marketplace, and there he saw one he knew very well: his father's car. His heart jumped but he made himself go over for a close look. Inside, a familiar old cushion and a home-covered road map confirmed this fear. Not waiting for the heavy hand on the shoulder, he rode off at speed.

A noisy hen party was in progress. Morris instantly regretted his wild arrival. They all stared at him.

"Morris?"

"Mum, can you come a minute."

Her bright society smile died. She and Bea exchanged looks; Bea shrugged. "Go on, Annie."

Outside, Morris announced, "Dad's here."

Her hands clutched at nothing. "Here?"

"In the town. I saw the car."

"And him? Did you see him?"

"No, but it still is his car; I looked inside."

"How long ago? God, he doesn't know we're here, does he?" She wanted to pace about but the hall was too confined.

"I came straight back," Morris said.

She nodded. "He'll think we're at Patrick's—why did I tell him that much? Oh, don't look so sulky; help me, Morris."

"Well, we don't have to be on the run from Dad, do we?" he demanded. "It's stupid, this carry-on."

She glanced at the door as if expecting ears bulging through the woodwork. "Ssh; oh what . . . just go and tell Bea I want her a minute. I can't."

He did so. He could tell from the unnatural hush that they'd been making dramatic faces over his mother's case.

Bea slipped out to them importantly.

"Matthew's here."

"Oh Annie, where? How do you know?"

"He's in town; Morris saw the car."

"Only the car? Maybe—"

"No, I don't doubt it's him. Oh Bea, I can't—"

Bea put her arms round Annie, muttering angry and gentle things in her ear. "Morris," she said, "don't just stand there, go inside and tell them I'll be back in a few minutes."

"In *there*, with *them?*"

She glared. "In a *few minutes.*" (God, how alike women were!) "Come on, Annie, let's go upstairs."

64   Morris put as little of himself into the room as pos-

sible, poised for flight. He said rapidly, "Bea says she'll be back in a few minutes."

All the heads turned toward him like lilies to the light. A voice asked, "Is your mother all right?"

"Sure."

"Can I help?" from another.

"No thanks." He would have fled but for a plate of appetizers and a large, sliced fruitcake. "Excuse me," he said, and grabbed.

Halfway up the stairs he tripped over Kelly the spy. Sensible of her mother and his nearby, he tried to pass silently, but she fastened onto his ankle and held on, even when he kicked out.

"What do you want?" he demanded.

"Oh wait. Don't go up there, somebody's crying."

"I know, it's my mum; let go."

"Why did you have to come here? It was all right till you came."

Her face was truly miserable. "We'll be gone directly," he said. "Now let go."

"I don't like it."

"*I* don't like it," Morris agreed. He had a sudden vision of the dramatic scene as his father arrived, with all the hens having a wonderful time. Kelly let go his ankle and he passed upstairs. There was no sound of weeping now. He looked down at the little girl, who was twisted round to watch him.

He gave her a thumbs-up sign and a very brief grin.

8

t took a long time, with nothing to do but lie on a bed and think, before Morris could quiet his mind. The thing with his father was out of his hands, in this place, with Bea and Co. taking over. He didn't know how he felt about it. It was easier to dream of the setup, to slot himself into it. And poor Miss Farmhouse.

He recalled the new name he would have given her: Vail. She'd have said, "Thank you, Lord," and made that quaint sign with her hands. *We could have done a lot. I could have helped her work the rebels as their mysterious leader. We could have blown up one of the towers, perhaps recruited from inside the castle, formed a real guerrilla army. If I get the chance to go there again . . . why not, even without her?*

God, I wonder when I'll get a proper meal; I'm bloody starving.

| | | | | | | | | | | |

In the morning, with no visit from her wicked husband, Annie Nelson simply sat and repeated like a recorded message, "We'll be leaving this house in peace within the next twenty-four hours." She plainly hadn't slept well.

"Where are we going now?" Morris asked her.

"To a friend's."

"You could stay here, Annie, except—" Bea didn't say what.

"Why can't we go home?" Morris demanded.

"It's Christmas," his mother announced sadly. "I'm not spending it all alone in that miserable house. Christmas is supposed to be a family time, and my family's here." Bea looked uncomfortable. "So why can't Matt just leave us alone?"

"If we went home," Morris said, "he would leave us alone, same as he's been doing for all the rest of the year."

Bea glanced from one to the other, not used to the game.

Annie turned suddenly fiery. "I wonder, Morris, why I bother with you. Perhaps I *should* have left you there by yourself—what difference would it have made to you? You don't know one day from the next, you're just like your father—leave home and after five months he thought it was only as many weeks—" She turned to Bea. "He did that, you know, and this one's the same. He doesn't care, so why should I?"

Morris hunched his shoulders and muttered, "That's not true."

The front door rattled; they all stiffened, then, "It's the mail," Bea said brightly.

Morris declared, "I'm going out," to follow Bea before any more could be said.

"Where? Oh Morris, look, don't just run out."

"You hurt me." He paused by the door. She said no more. She opened her hands to entreat him; he would have relented, but Bea was suddenly back between them, showing off the Christmas cards in her hand.

The moment destroyed, Morris said, "See you later," and left.

Since he had no other place to go to, he went to the station, telling himself: *If there's a useful train soon I'll get it and go to East Lodge. Screw getting back.* In fact the useful train was due so very soon that he convinced himself it was the fated thing to do. Problems such as getting into the house would doubtless be solved as easily.

Of course no one answered the doorbell, because Patrick must be at work. *Well*, Morris told himself, *I've tried that. And Patrick did say* (rattling the back door) *I was welcome any time. As long as I didn't touch the wrong things. And this* (standing on an old packing case to force a likely window) *isn't one of the wrong things; it held my weight and the window opens, which just proves it.*

Once inside the house Morris went directly upstairs, never doubting now that he could gain entry to the setup. The door was locked. Naturally. The key would be waiting for him. And so it was. Simple.

It was only when he was finally standing in the room, surveying his conquest, that he realized what a remote victory it was; for now he was here, what could he do? Nothing, nothing. The most beautiful

68 temptation imaginable, and all the magic of its control

was unknown to him. Not that he'd needed any technology to talk with Vail.

Now if she'd be there, I could tell her her new name, and then work out a plan of attack . . .

Morris was sorry for betraying her, then angry with Patrick for having tricked him so easily, then empty with the sense of muddle and loss that seemed to be washing over him too often these past weeks or months.

I've got to do something. Think. Vail, the other figures, in the box—where did he put them? Somewhere, just chucked aside. If I could put Vail back into her home, maybe she'd warm up, come back to life.

He started to poke among the considerable debris discarded against the walls. The lighting wasn't very good, shadowed and dusty. He found pieces of scenery, small and large, none very convincing (how did they grow so real, once in place?). He found plenty of boxes, mostly bearing serial numbers but empty, with or without lids. One box, beneath much clutter, exposed a jumble of drab, rejected model figures. He knew at once they were not the ones he'd been looking for.

Some were human, some monstrous. So at one time Patrick must have played a sword-and-sorcery game, the kind Morris understood, little heroes against magical monsters and demons. Now these poor creatures were forgotten and thrown away. And now the latest cast-offs—

"Hello," Ian said, "how did you get in?" showing a door key on his open palm.

Morris blinked and gulped.

"No windows broken," Ian hoped.

"No."

"Good. I let you in, did I."

As it didn't sound like a question, Morris tried for a grateful grin. He felt more foolish than he'd believed possible.

Ian came across to see what he was holding. He nodded. "Put that back," he advised. "Anywhere underneath'll do." He scanned the setup, checking it against the intruder. "Do you like taking risks?" he asked.

"Patrick did say I could come, any time."

"Surely. On certain terms, I think. Over here; come and be useful." No more questions. What a pity more people weren't like Ian. He introduced Morris to a very few simple effects: how to create day and night, sunshine and threatened storm, how to use the monitor. Small gifts that were never to be misused.

"Now," Ian said, "since things are still not right, I'm going to test them out. Taking out those figures was not the answer, so the trouble must be something else we've overlooked. Can't have the natives sulking, can we?" He grinned knowingly. "So we'll try a real all-action assault, strong sunlight, monitor set to Castle, North Approach. Set them at that weakened main door again. Now we'll see."

One second the area opposite the great doors was empty, the next it was studded with assorted waiting peasants.

70 "See?" Ian said. "Look at them, a bunch of medieval layabouts."

"Who commands them?" Morris asked.

"We do."

"No, who's their leader?"

"That's us. We say 'go,' and they go. Pan along a bit, Morris. Lord, what a crew!"

"What's that?" Morris turned suddenly from the screen in wonder. "A *cannon*? Is that right?"

"Bombard, early type, authentic. Now then, lads, get to it."

The little figures around the gun busied themselves for a minute; there was a surprisingly loud report, a lot of smoke and flame, and a shower of debris from a hole in the road in front of the castle.

While the bombard's crew stood back in a resigned group, several heads appeared along the top of the castle wall. They looked down at the new crater with unhurried interest.

Ian moaned in despair. "Look at that!" he cried. "Can you believe it? Did I say 'high-action assault'? Look at them go! What excitement!"

Morris said, "But if you're in command, can't you make them push on, or the castle troops fire at them, or something?"

"It's preprogrammed," Ian said. "Now the attackers follow up (that shot was supposed to breach the doors) and in the panic and confusion force the defenders out into the open. You see?"

They squatted down in comfort, since the battle was apparently going to take some time.

The peasant army now ambled forward into the road. Several went to gape at the crater. Ian started chewing his nails.

Some sound effects started up: a warning shout from the gun crew, a ragged answer from the ranks, a thin trumpet call from the castle. *At last*, Morris hoped.

The peasants closed up, the bombard fired again.

"No!" Ian groaned. "Move the bloody thing first, you wimps!"

A second crater appeared, this time in the grass a little nearer the castle wall. The attackers shifted forward with an uninspired shout, their weapons carried like walking sticks. Then they foregathered in front of the gates and waited, politely.

"It's rubbish," Ian observed. "They've got to get those doors opened, it's programmed."

From the high battlements, the trumpeter and a couple of shining knights peered over at the deputation. Faintly, as on a distant breeze, the sound of a shouted conversation between the two groups could be heard. Ian jumped up and spun a switch to amplify the sound to maximum. (*Is that how I heard Vail speaking?* Morris wondered.) Now all they heard clearly was "So be it!" from the battlements, followed by quite a pleasant laugh.

After a pause (the deputation waited in silence), muffled voices from behind the doors announced the unmistakable groan of bolts being slowly withdrawn.

One door opened a little; a man in full armor came out, alone, and held out his empty hands. The peasants stared at him dumbly.

"Is it a trick?" Morris whispered.

72   "God knows."

(*Aren't you God? Don't you know?*)

First one, then two, then three more of the peasants loped up to the knight with their hands outstretched. They touched fingers in turn and passed singly through the gate. The knight followed the last one, the door shut behind him.

The rest of the peasant army seemed to fade and melt back into the landscape.

"How do they change color like that?" Morris asked.

Ian shook his head, but not aware of the question. "Now you've seen it too," he said. "So what do we do next?"

"What does Patrick think?" Morris asked.

"He's not pleased, to put it mildly."

"What will he do if it can't be put right?"

"Play hell with the manufacturers—or chuck it all in."

"Chuck it in? *This?*" Morris couldn't believe it. "But it's—"

"Oh, don't worry." Ian grinned. "He'll find something else. That's how he is—in fact, that reaction wouldn't surprise me at all."

"But what would happen to this?"

Ian shrugged. "Part exchange maybe. Or he'll incorporate some of it into another setup as he's done before. He's very clever, you know. This sort of annoyance'll challenge him for a while, but if it doesn't sort out he'll turn to something new. It keeps you awake. Next time you come visiting, hey presto, all this'll be gone and there'll be—" He shrugged and went away to play with the console.

9

Morris couldn't bear such sanity. He wandered down the room to the cluster of farm buildings. The one that Patrick had kicked had been patched up, but carelessly; the stones didn't fit, with unmortared gaps between.

He asked Ian, "Where do the figures go, when they've finished a game, like now?"

"Wherever they've been programmed," Ian said, "usually home base."

"How do they get there?"

"Magic." Ian was busy, not paying attention. Morris got down to squint inside the repaired cottage. It was certainly occupied. *So what about . . .* he went, quietly and casually, to look inside the little building that had hidden the four renegades. It was plainly empty. Those four hadn't been absorbed by the castle, so they hadn't been resurrected. A weight passed down Morris's throat to lodge in his chest. He didn't want to see in there anymore.

To conceal his misery, he kept down low, making as if to look into all the buildings. *You silly dollies,* he thought; *you suppose you're being clever with your go-slow tactics, but you're just irritating God, and if you don't entertain he'll rub you out. Now if* I *could take control* . . .

Staring hard at the wall of a building, he became aware of a figure pressed like a dappled moth against it. One optical illusion shifted into the next, the body camouflaged, the eyes widely staring, at him. The gaze connected; they knew each other. "Vail," his mouth formed, and "Farmhouse," it whispered.

Impossibly, the lids lowered and lifted once, the face that was a mask became a secret smile.

How was this possible when Vail was dead and cast away in a shared coffin? Still she looked at him, that singular expression.

Morris whispered, "Wait," and moved quietly back to Ian. "You know that box with the models in that Patrick took out—where is it?"

Ian's mind was deep into other things. "Over there somewhere," he said absently, adding, more sharply, "Didn't you find it then?"

Looking where Ian had pointed, Morris did find the box, very easily. Wary of doing anything forbidden, he took it to Ian and asked his permission to take the figures out.

Ian said, "Sure," and poked at the models with one finger. "Just put them back, after."

Back at the far end of the room Morris sat with his back to the wall and put the box on the floor.

The figures were so cold and stiff, so modeled, that it was impossible to believe they had ever moved with that spine-creeping fluidity he himself had witnessed. 75 He deliberately took up a little man first, not trusting his casual appearance. He turned it over, seeking some clue as to how it could have moved; a ridge joining parts together or any signs of contact points. It was so finely made that he found nothing.

Its peasant clothes were modeled in such detail that there was even a cleverly stitched patch on the sleeve. The expression on the face was of weary death, the overall color an unpainted dun.

Morris put the little man on the floor, upright. He stood on solid, well-balanced feet in a posture of ageless resignation. There was nothing warlike about him. Morris felt such a sweep of pity that he took the figure up again and laid it back in the box, in case— how silly—in case the poor creature's soul had looked out from behind its imprisoning shell, sick for life and its homeland.

His hands shook as he lifted out the little dead female; so much that he had to hold her without looking for a very long minute. She didn't warm in his hand or become plastic, even in the imagination.

At last, he looked, through a fog afflicting his eyes. She was one of a set with the male peasant; the same noncolor, composition, standard of fine modeling. Dressed in long robes with a hood part concealing her face. Morris guessed that all the male peasants would be one set of clones, and all the females another set, perhaps with differing superficial details.

This one was Farmhouse kin, but not Vail. Vail was alive, waiting for his word. This creature was dead, a relic. At this comfortable standpoint, his mind took shelter and settled.

Ian wandered down to see what he was doing. He took the figure from Morris and examined it admiringly. "They're very good, faulty or not," he said.

"How do they work?" Morris asked.

"There's a question."

"If we put those back—"

"Not for me to decide," Ian said. "How did you know *these* were our villains?"

"I thought. I—watched them," Morris mumbled.

"Ah. Yes. Bad girl." He let the figure drop into the box. "Patrick'll be home any time now. I'm going down to sort us out some food. What about you?"

"Can I stay here? I won't touch anything." A look passed between them.

Ian raised a hand, and left him alone.

When the footsteps had decidedly faded down the stairs, Morris went quickly back to see if Vail was still waiting by the wall. He took the box with him.

She hadn't moved, barely visible, beautifully camouflaged against the mottled stone.

He lifted the female figure out of the box and placed it on the floor; just outside the edge of her home ground, facing him. Now, by careful alignment, he could see both faces at the same time; both alike, one dead, one very much alive. It was nice to feel he hadn't hurt *her* after all. This one didn't matter. On a sharp impulse, he swiveled the dead one round to face her sister: the distance between them was not great. It was a cruel pleasure to see her eyes widen with simple horror; and then he was sorry, but too late.   77

Her faraway voice said, "Lord, I must go on, whatever punishment you show me."

Morris said, "Was she a Farmhouse, too?"

"My kin." Her eyes fixed in compassion, her cheeks so pale.

"Listen," Morris said, "I'm calling you Vail from now on, not Farmhouse. You're individual, different from the rest."

She looked at him briefly, and back at the other. "Your hands are mine," she said. "I will follow to the end."

He said, "But what are you doing?"

She answered, "Why, Lord, nothing contrary. And your design begins to work, you see; some are won over and we shall surely triumph over the empty-headed."

It was dangerous talk, as from a religious revolutionary. She was a very strange peasant.

"Don't you want to get into the castle?" Morris asked.

Her face lit with a smile. "You know we do," she said. "But the old stories of its cruelty and wickedness have poisoned us for too long. Jealousy of beauty and anger are very wrong."

Morris agreed, though he had no idea what she was talking about. Old stories? Among a set of computerized games pieces? "Tell me one of your stories," he said.

She looked at him as if to say: You're teasing me. *Of course*, he thought; *as God I'm supposed to know them.*

"In a time before linked memory," she related, "when the Forest was only the West Village garden, the kin that lived there always boasted that they, they alone, were under the castle's protection, living so close to it. They let it be known that their villagers passed freely in and *out* of the castle; a great honor. Then came the day when all the village kin danced in through their private door—the small Westgate—with songs and flowers, laughing; but only one came out, mad and horribly dismembered, to tell how all the innocents had been betrayed and made to suffer most cruelly before their end. Only he had been cast back, as witness to the power of the castle's darkness."

Morris felt he'd always known that tale, or snatches of it. He asked her, "Who told you that?"

She said, "It is true that there was once a village where the Forest stands, you can feel the ruins of its buildings like covered furniture under the grass. But no one ever comes out of the castle who goes in it. That part, the wounded man's horror, cannot be true. It is a tale to frighten new kin, to keep them angry and afraid. *I* don't believe it."

"And how will it be different when you get into the castle?" Morris asked.

"See," she said. She raised her hands slowly, palms outward. She smiled gravely, saying, "I come in peace and love." Then the smile changed to a grin and her voice lightened. "You mustn't doubt us," she said. "I'm not alone, and we all know where our feet and butts are."

After the first shock, Morris sat back on his heels and laughed aloud.

"Good lord," Patrick said from the doorway, "has it got you as bad as that? What's the joke?"

"Oh—just thoughts." Morris stood up quickly, with a sly couple of side shuffles away from the danger area.

"You want to eat?" Patrick asked. "There's stuff out downstairs."

"Thanks." And a few casual steps up and down.

"We'll have another go at this after. Leave the lights."

Mechanically eating, Morris's mind ran over and over that weird conversation, the legend of a people who were not people and couldn't possibly have legends. Those computer programs must be something really special.

Suddenly Patrick called, "Hi, dreamboy, you in love or something?" and he and Ian laughed.

"What?" Face stupidly burning.

"Do you want to go back up, or are you too old for my kind of toys?" Patrick said.

Morris moved so quickly he bumped a chair over.

"We won't be long," Patrick said, "just a few more details to go over. You're free to work the switches you know, but leave the rest, won't you."

Perhaps, Morris thought, *I am in love; or I've taken the stairs too fast.* His heart seemed in danger of dislodging the hand flat on his chest.

He tried the monitor, but was frustrated by his own clumsy attempts to find the right area, let alone one single figure. So he went back to kneel in the same place as before, where Vail's poor abandoned sister was still staring blindly out over her lost homeland. Ashamed, he took and laid her gently to rest with her kin in the box.

Vail had rightly interpreted the sight of her dead sister as: This dreadful fate could be yours. She was waiting for him, as he had commanded, watching his every move. Now she detached herself from the sheltering wall, saying simply, "Here I am."

"Vail," Morris said, "listen: it would be better if you and your mates lie low for a while. If you don't, it's more than likely you'll never get into that castle."

She gave it thought. "Lord, I hear. None of us are afraid for ourselves. We are one mind. Where one fails, another will succeed. A bad end for one or two is nothing."

Morris said, "But suppose the *whole thing* should end?"

"Lord?"

"Your whole world. End, be destroyed."

"The Apocalypse?" She waited for him to deny it. "That cannot be, Lord," she said firmly, "we're nowhere near the prophecy."

"What prophecy?"

" 'The Land shall break apart with the Five Terrors ...' That alone cannot be while kin work together to a common cause."

"What are the Five Terrors?" Morris asked.

She tilted her head slightly with that you're-testing-me-again look. "They can't happen," she assured him, "not all five; only Sleep worries me sometimes—"

"Sleep?"

"The Second Terror, Sleep."

"I don't—"

"Well, Morris," a voice boomed behind him, "what are you doing, saying your prayers?"

He scrambled to his feet blindly as his worlds collided. "Dad?"

"Who else? Well, I'm glad you're glad to see me." Morris grinned nervously.

"And how are you?"

"All right."

"Enjoying this?" His father laughed as he surveyed the setup. "If I told them at work about this, they'd never believe me. Amazing. That's what you can do—" with a hand on Morris's shoulder— "when all your goods are your own. Clever, your uncle Pat."

"I know."

"I was here last night—couldn't resist another look."

Last night, Morris's mind chewed; when we were all being miserable. It was hard not to snarl. "It's been a long time since we've seen you," he said.

"I know, I've not had a moment. Sorry. Anyway—"

"You couldn't be that busy," Morris objected.

"Well. Anyway, with Christmas coming up—"

Morris looked away, disgusted. Was that all: Santa Claus time? "Mum's not here," he said. "She's at Bea's."

"Yes, I know."

"Are you going over there?"

"I wanted to see you first."

"Oh yes? Nobody knew I was here?"

"I took a chance. Pat told me how knocked out you were by all this."

He didn't believe, yet wanted to. "Why did you want to see me first?" he asked.

"To find out what my chances are."

Turning aside, unable to get himself together, Morris briefly wondered if Vail was watching and listening to this elevated discussion between the gods. Or did her mind switch off . . .

"Dammit, Morris," his father suddenly exploded, "won't you listen to me?"

"Sorry. Go on." Surely she couldn't hear them . . .

"It's Christmas; do you think that hasn't hurt, being without you?"

"Only now?" Morris had to say.

They both looked away. "I couldn't let it go on," his father said. "I had to come and see you. You promised to keep in touch, Morris, and how long is it—well, never mind. I think about you a lot, you know, about that school—how's math, by the way?" Morris shrugged. "And surely you never thought I'd forget to bring you something for Christmas?" A false grin.

"I don't need anything," Morris said. It sounded petty, when he'd meant it to be politely matter-of-fact.

"Oh, come on. If it embarrasses you, I've left the parcels downstairs, here. Save them till the twenty-fifth, like we used to do."

Oh, don't, don't. "Parcels?" Morris said. (*Oh, I can't think about what we used to do.*)

83

"For your mother as well. Why not?" Another bluff smile.

"I hope it's nothing she can throw at me and smash in pieces," Morris said, a feeble joke.

"Oh no, I thought of that."

"Or anything sexy—who chose it?"

"I did of course, who else?"

"Your other woman."

The immediate silence was physically painful. *Go on*, Morris's mind urged, *deny it*; but his father said nothing.

At last, Morris muttered, "Thanks, anyway. I'm sorry, I haven't got you anything."

"No matter, I didn't expect it."

"Are you going to see Mum now?"

"Possibly—what do you think? Help me, Morris."

"Oh, don't ask me. But I'm warning you, Cousin Bea'll give you hell if she sees you, and so will all the other hens hanging around there."

"Women's Front, hey?" With a tiny flicker of life, they laughed ruefully together. *Like we used to do. How long ago . . .*

"Morris, I want us to be friends," his father said quickly.

"Yes. And we're leaving that house tomorrow, I think," Morris added before he changed his mind. "I don't know where we're going, to some friend's; she won't go home. It's *Christmas* time and we've got to have fun." Like lemon shriveling the mouth. "So you'll have to hurry up whatever you're going to do, or forget it." *Please, please.*

"Thanks," his father said. He struggled for more, but it wouldn't come. He reached out and gripped Morris's arms, almost pulling him into an embrace. "I'll see you," he said. "Take care."

"You too."

This is the way the gods talk.

10

Vail was gone. Not silently camouflaged awaiting his attention; gone, away, while the big boys were squabbling. If he'd dared, Morris too would have kicked in the nearest little building. Very faintly, he could hear voices downstairs, then a called goodbye. Was Dad really off to face Cousin Bea's fire? In a way, he'd like to see that, but safely, on a secret monitor.

Remembering Vail's "old story," he went around to look at the castle from the west, the forest side. Standing, he could see the doorway that she'd called the Westgate. It was tucked into a dogleg section of outer wall, like a door to a hidden garden. So he lay flat, for a model's-eye view of it through the trees.

The doorway was almost obscured now, but —he caught his breath—he perceived how the forest floor here was unnaturally bumpy, exactly as she'd said, like shrouded furniture. The ruins of an old village?

He stood up again to peer over the trees at the secret door. The castle was very close to the trees, with only a path and a narrow strip of no-man's-land between them.

Across the room, Patrick and Ian were watching him. Their deeply thoughtful faces made his heart sink. He waved cheerfully and called for them to come.

"Do you make attacks from here?" he asked when they were beside him.

"I think there is one." Patrick squatted and squinted through the trees.

"Only one?" Morris said. "But it'd be perfect, wouldn't it, with the trees so near to the walls for cover, and that little door unguarded."

Ian went at once to bring the view up close on the monitor. And there was the door, fast set, with iron hinges and a huge drop-handle. Silver-edged ivy trailed right across it from the wall.

"We've never breached that door," Ian murmured.

"But why not? As Morris says—let's set it up, now."

While they worked out the plan, Morris studied the door left on the screen. It was as if the dimension barrier was gone; he was of a size to enter that door, if only he knew how to open it—and had the courage. You must take the handle in both hands and pull the door toward you. At the same time Vail must insert the precious key and turn anti-clockwise. The lock clicks dully; turn again, release the pull, open the door. The ivy will bend back.

Inside, a narrow alleyway, right and left, fronted by another, higher wall with plants growing between the cracks. "Bitter starwort," Vail says. It creeps also across the path, unhindered by any feet. No one comes this way.

The alley curves to the shape of the castle itself. A second door, unused, opens to the same key, and inside is a small eccentric courtyard surrounded by high, sunless walls. There is a sunk well off center, covered by a grid, which cannot prevent the rising scent of decay. This was the foolish villagers' dancingplace; their cries racket from wall to wall; at each slit window a privileged onlooker smiles down as the dances turn to trapped panic, the songs to shrieks of horror. *Vail, you're wrong, come away, come away!* Why didn't she understand?

His shoulder was being shaken hard, a voice was shouting in his ear. It was Patrick, telling him to wake up and watch the show. Ian, behind him, was looking warily anxious.

"Come on," Patrick said, "it's your idea, basically; we've set it up and it's ready to run."

"I don't think—" Morris faltered, and, "I ought to go home."

Patrick and Ian exchanged significant glances. "This won't take long," Patrick said.

"Then I'll take you," Ian added. "Look, it's started already."

The picture on the screen drew back to show a group of peasants sitting on the bank at the edge of the trees. As they waited, the light gently dimmed to a rosy winter sunset, spotlighting the door in the wall.

That was clever. Morris began to be interested.

The view shifted, as a solitary figure, a young man, came through the trees from the north toward the others. Some turned their heads but only one stood up to greet him. They made as if to shake hands, but, "Ah," Ian breathed, "see, something's changed hands there; he gave her something."

Her? Turn around, Morris prayed, let me see your face. The two stood, heads bowed, a moment, and then she did turn. If it wasn't Vail it was one of her kin. He didn't know what to hope for.

The two came to the rest and she held out her hands. Ian zoomed in: it was a large, iron key.

"Turn up the sound," Patrick murmured.

"I have," Ian answered, "they're not talking. A solemn moment, evidently."

The two went first across the path and up to the unguarded door. The rest got up slowly, lagging behind. The go-slow looked to be still in operation. Or perhaps they were afraid. Ian followed the leaders closely, fixed on their hands, to see how they would treat with the door. Just as Morris had known, the young man held and pulled the handle, while the woman inserted and turned the key. The door opened slowly but without trouble. Still the followers hung behind, but the pair ignored them and passed through into the alleyway without even a glance back.

"Can we follow?" Patrick asked Ian.

"Not very well," Ian answered. The picture was already grainy and slightly out of focus. "I can't keep close to them," he said. "They'll be out of range in a minute."

Morris had noted the strange plant creeping from the cracks in the walls. The knowledge of what was to come was like leaden guilt inside.

The picture changed back to the group of unwilling peasants still outside the first door. "The door's open, why don't they go in?" Patrick wondered. "They're programmed to go in, aren't they, Ian?"

"Supposedly," Ian agreed without conviction.

"Damn thing," Patrick muttered, "value for money, my backside; I'm not putting up with this much longer."

Oh, do something! Morris urged the army silently; *don't leave it all to the first two. And what's happening to them now?*

There was some kind of noise from inside the wall, eerie and thin; possibly a signal, for the peasants regrouped themselves into a tight wedge, pushing forward a very reluctant frontman right up to the door. Since he had no choice, he stepped through and peered to right and left down the alleyway. Silently, the others followed.

As soon as they were all through the door, Ian was forced to face up to the problem of keeping the monitor with them. No close-ups were possible. "Ah," he breathed, "here's the inner door; now then, can we get through ...?" The image dived, dissolved, and re-formed. "That's the best I can do," he said finally. "Rotten, but the first time we've been so far into the works."

"What is it?" Patrick squinted at the fuzzy picture.

"Some kind of yard, nothing there, well that's exciting; where are all our merry lads? What's that splodge over to the right?"

"It's a well," Morris said.

"Is it? Could be, I suppose. Where are those dim-wits? Ian, can't you just—"

"Sorry, no. They'll be out of the picture, prowling around; we'll just have to wait—there, look."

Something vaguely recognizable as a figure loomed into sight and away, like a fish in a dim aquarium. Then there were several in a bunch by the splodge that Morris claimed was a well. They stayed there a minute and then shot off at a surprising rate.

"They don't care for that, whatever it is," Patrick murmured. "Have we got it in the plan, Ian? What about in the handbook?"

"Not sure about that," Ian answered. "I'll look it up after."

It was the first Morris had heard about a handbook. He thought he'd like to look at it too.

More thin, layered sounds pierced the silence. Ian rushed to adjust the controls, but shook his head. Morris shut his eyes as the sounds shivered right through him: the cries of absolute terror and pain: the betrayed.

"Look at them go!" Patrick said. Morris opened his eyes to see the screen blurred with panic as figures rushed for the door. Ian didn't follow them; instead, he left the view as it was until the screen was empty once more. Not quite empty; there was now another splodge over to the left, and an addition to the origi-nal. They watched. The new splodge moved a little and wiggled hopelessly toward the camera; then it collapsed and was still. The other splodge made no movement at all.

"Bodies," Patrick said. "What got them?"

"The crush, probably," Ian said.

The watchers waited. Something wispy drifted across the screen and appeared to collect itself in a cloud above each body, after which it swarmed into one mass and funneled into the well.

"Ghosts," stated Morris.

Patrick glanced at him sideways.

Now other forms, vague but solid, edged into view, to attend to the bodies. "The cleanup brigade," Ian said. "Those two are for recycling." As they were dragged off, he changed the picture, reversing into the alleyway, through the Westgate and out into the path at the forest's edge. By some means the sunset had been arrested, so that the world outside seemed suddenly clear and clean, a place to breathe in.

"Now," Patrick said sternly, "where are they? Didn't we forbid them to run off? Aha." And there they were, the sorry peasant band, resting among the trees like Robin Hood's not-so-merry men after a hard day's pillage.

"They want to go home," Ian said. "Look at their miserable faces."

"Stupid, not miserable," Patrick said.

"Why can't they go home?" Morris asked.

"Because we haven't finished with them yet. *We're* here to play games with *them*, not the other way round. Come on, my lads, rally-ho."

One or two slowly got up, watching the still-open doorway, but there was nothing to see, no likelihood of any action. Bored and annoyed, Patrick went over for a consultation with Ian. They held a large, floppy book between them, turning pages, baffled, unable to agree. This must be the handbook, and in it, the mythology.

Morris got down to look at the peasants' level. They were static again. Beyond them, Vail was standing alone in the doorway, facing the cowards, facing him. He wondered if she saw his face, like a low full moon between the trees. She gave no sign.

Ian and Patrick were busy, their backs to him. Daring all, Morris gingerly inserted one hand vertically among the trees, moving as slowly as an intently prowling cat, not touching anything, weight on the other hand. Then he stopped, transferred his gaze to her face, and gently moved his fingers. He was sure now that he had her attention. Carefully, he withdrew his hand.

She was looking at him, but the distance was too great to speak. It was silly, but he simply wanted her to know he was there. He glanced once more at the two busy with their plans, and when he looked back, he was surprised to see that Vail had moved, so quickly that she was already some way into the trees toward him. Even as he watched, she glided on, until there was only a narrow band of cover between them. None of the peasants had turned around; she alone seemed to have the power of self-movement.

She looked up at him and raised her hands in greet- 93

ing. He dared a small smile but was afraid to speak. She did not smile: he remembered where she'd just been, and understood. The "old story" she'd scorned had been proved a likely truth after all.

"Thank you, Lord," she said.

Morris blinked, thinking, *whatever for?* but not saying, because of Patrick. He appeared to have heard nothing.

"You put that way in into my mind, and lo, it's still open to us. We'll go back in, shortly, you'll see, but it's a gigantic step to take in one move."

Morris did his best to stay smiling. He gave an encouraging nod. It was obviously useless, bearing in mind the continuing program, to tell her not to do anything so foolish.

"The key," he mouthed carefully.

"It is safe, handed back."

"Don't be afraid," he breathed.

She put one hand to her mouth and extended the fingers toward him, an offering. Then she turned and glided back to her little company. Morris thought, *Like Joan of Arc, and just as daft.*

One by one they stood up, ready to go with her. He was pleased to see how they at least went in a close bunch together, not leaving her to go first and alone. The one who had helped her open the door seemed not to be there: maybe he was one of the two bodies. That pained Morris, who had been into that part himself.

As the group passed reluctantly into the alleyway, Ian suddenly noticed and called Patrick's attention.

The screen was quickly brought into play. "They don't want to go in again, do they?" Ian observed. "It's very odd."

"It must be, according to the handbook, the Massacre Myth," Patrick said.

"We should have read up on it," Ian said, "taken it into account before setting them on; we'll be wasting it if it's a dead end."

Patrick made a moan of disgust. "Strikes me there's altogether too many dead ends built into this setup; it's a dead loss."

"We should have read up on it," Ian said again. "If we want them to really charge into this, the program directives'll have to be a whole lot stronger. We could, you know—next time."

"How about override?"

Ian shook his head. With no great hopes, they settled to watch events. The peasants had arrived at the inner door but were not willing to proceed any further.

Patrick went to the console, muttering, twitching his fingers between keyboard and switches. Ian stayed with the monitor. Patrick said, "See what *that* does," and rubbed his hands together as if they were cold.

It seemed that some sudden resolution had fired the little band. Now eager to re-enter the scene of panic, they thrust themselves forward, propelled like wasps in a bottle-trap. Vail was quite lost among them.

Ian was having the same trouble as before in getting a clear picture, but Patrick didn't interfere: Ian was the technical expert. Surely, Morris thought, Patrick could just stride up to the castle itself and look over the wall into the courtyard—better than getting so worked up with a rotten secondhand view on a screen. Yet he didn't do it.

In the yard, there was a great commotion. Blurred figures passed and repassed in a wild sort of chaindance. There were sounds, too, like suppressed chanting. Either they were reenacting the original story, or working themselves up to a brave attack. Or, of course, they were simply little games pieces under the influence of a strong program. Suddenly they all disappeared from view, with only the sound thinning away to indicate their continued movement.

Patrick looked hopelessly at Ian, but he said, "No, sorry, there's no way I can follow them in there."

"Where've they gone?" Morris asked.

"Right into the castle building," Ian said. "They've really done it at last, got right inside."

"But how? Did they bash down the doors, or what? Did the knights let them?"

"Knights," Patrick scoffed. "But what's the use if we can't follow to see what happens?"

"You know what happens," Ian reminded him. "They'll all get eaten up and resurrected. There's nothing *to* see in there."

"What is the castle like inside?" Morris asked.

"Don't know," Patrick admitted crossly. "It's a closed component. Probably hollow except for the works and storage. You'd think you could fit up a camera—"

"Not unless you open it up," Ian said.

"Can of worms," Patrick muttered.

Morris stared at the great building as longingly as its owner. It wasn't possible for him to imagine it as a hollow shell: there must be narrow passages, stone spiral staircases, echoing halls, and—surely—dark dungeons, in there. A place for the knights to relax and the band to practice, another place for the grim cleanup brigade to do their work and the new kin to be re-formed. Death and resurrection. No, not just an empty box.

Patrick was getting more and more irritated. His frustration had shifted from the supposed malfunction among the peasants to the inner workings of the castle. Now he was arguing with Ian as to how they could fix up something to view those inner workings.

"If this is all we can do," Patrick concluded, "then I've had enough of it."

"I can't see how it would work," Ian protested. "You could ruin the whole setup."

"So." Patrick shrugged. "It's a dead loss as it is, and if I'm willing to take the risk, that's it."

"It's your money," Ian said.

"Right." Patrick suddenly turned to Morris. "What do you think, hey? Shall we take the edifice to pieces—well, drill a few holes for a bit of micro-surgery? Kill or cure?"

Morris said, "But I don't know anything about it." (*Vail's in there, beyond reach.*)

"Oh come on," Patrick urged, "you don't have to know anything to see what a dead bore it is. As a layman, an interested party, what do you think? Shall 97 we go in?" He grinned. "Look at his face," he said to Ian. "There's no need to answer, of course he wants in."

(*What's happening to her now? In a ground-floor dungeon like an aircraft hangar, in a cage or on a slab . . .*) Morris looked at Ian. "I would like to see some real action," he said.

Ian blinked, drew a quick breath, and glanced at his watch. "So you will, if I don't get you back home right now."

"Home?"

Ian grabbed Morris's sleeve, saying, "Come on, sleepwalker." And as they left, he promised Patrick, "All right, squire, you win. Work on it, I'll see you tomorrow."

Patrick was already scattering papers all over the floor.

11

an drove for some time in silence. Morris meanwhile was gathering himself together for dra-
matics with his mother. He had no doubts that
his father had gone straight from East Lodge to
see her, with god knows what results.

"I should have gone back before," he said.

"It's not late," Ian said.

"No, I mean, with Dad haring off like he did.
I expect he went to see Mom. I didn't think, and
then I forgot about it."

Ian didn't comment straight away. Then he
said, "If he was going to see her anyway, you
were possibly best out of the way."

Morris hoped this was true. "He shouldn't
have come," he said. "All that stuff about Christmastime."

"It's a time makes people think again," Ian
said.

"Only for a day or two. All this pretty-
pretty—" they were passing through the deco-
rated marketplace—"it's all overrated. Like people who give puppies for Christmas presents and
throw them out in January." Like Patrick, he

99

thought suddenly, with all that marvelous stuff and he gets in a tantrum with it.

Ian said, "I wish I could help you."

Morris looked right away, out into the night. Genuinely kind people were worse than anything. "I tell you what I'd like to do," he said to the car window. "I'd like to be able to hide among those peasants, camouflaged exactly the same as the rest, so no one could find me."

"You'd get swallowed up and spat out by the castle," Ian joked. "Just think, you'd have to go on bashing away under orders, only to get eaten up and spat out, time after time after time."

"Just like real life," Morris said bitterly.

Ian said, "Ha-ha," without humor. They'd reached Cousin Bea's house, and he stopped the engine and switched off the lights. For a few minutes, they sat there in silence. Morris examined the lit but curtained windows for any sign of upheaval. He wasn't in a hurry to go in there.

At last Ian said: "It's possible I can help, though I may well be wrong. You tell me if you think I'm wrong—honestly, mind; I don't want to create havoc. The idea is, do you think your mother would let you spend Christmas with me and my mother? That's who I live with, you see; there's just the two of us, plus oddments on the Days—you could go and have any festivities with your own family any time you—she—likes." Morris couldn't speak, and Ian misinterpreted it. "Only I understood you and your mother were having some kind of difficulty over accommodation."

"Yes," Morris said.

"It was just an idea."

"It's great," Morris said, "but does your mother *know?* Wouldn't she mind? An old lady—"

"Good lord," Ian laughed, "that she isn't! How old do you think I am? I'm still the right side of thirty, I'd have you know."

"Sorry. Oh, are you sure?"

"Course. Do you want to ask what she says?"

"Now?"

"Why not?" Morris was already halfway out of the car. "Oh, one thing," Ian reminded him, "maybe we'd better leave any mention of Patrick out of this—am I right?"

Morris grinned and rushed up to the front door. Ian kept a little way back.

The door was opened by Kelly, before he'd even knocked. She must have been spying, as usual, and should, in any case, be in bed. She regarded Ian with suspicion and decided to ignore him.

"Your dad's been here," she whispered hoarsely.

"So what's new?" Morris whispered back.

"There's been a row."

"Surprise, surprise." It was horribly easy to slip back into the old role.

"He's gone now," she informed him. "My mum," with pride, "didn't half give him what-for."

"I bet."

"They were all over the house, up and down, shouting and swearing—"

"Is that you, Kelly? What are you doing?" came from the sitting room.

She pulled a face and didn't answer. The door opened and Cousin Bea came out to see for herself. "Morris," she said, beautifully rolled on the tongue. She glanced at Ian but left that for the moment. "Get to bed, Kelly," she said to her daughter, "and don't let me have to tell you again. I've more than enough to see to without that." A stern frown at Morris. She waited to make sure the little girl went upstairs before telling Morris once again that his father had been on a visit.

"I know," he said glumly. "*She* said."

"I think you knew before that," Bea said.

He didn't answer.

"You've been at East Lodge, haven't you." Bea included Ian in her glare.

"Mum said I could," Morris objected. "Ian here—" He stopped, before getting carried away. What had seemed so possible a few minutes ago now looked out of the question.

Ian said quietly, "I'd like to have a word with Mrs. Nelson, if I may."

Bea plainly mistrusted him, while not being too certain who he was. "She's not in any fit state to have words with anyone," she said. "Can't you tell me?" A quick glance toward Morris showed another layer of mistrust.

Ian did his best to smile. "I understand that Mrs. Nelson and Morris here have an accommodation problem for the next few days. I think I can help out, if she'll agree." He waited.

"How?" Bea asked. All exits were not yet closed.

"Morris can come and stay at my house, with me and my mother. We live fairly locally, just the two of us; he'd be very welcome."

Bea considered it. "And what about his mother?" she asked.

"Oh, I thought she had arrangements—I thought Morris was the problem," Ian said. Morris's heart sank.

"A problem," Bea agreed. Morris opened his mouth to protest, but shut it, at a nudge from Ian. It wasn't fair; he knew Bea had said his mother could stay on, by herself.

"Where is Mum?" he demanded.

"Recovering."

"Well ask her, *please*, just ask her," he pleaded.

Bea drew herself together, mouth tight shut. He wanted to punch her. Ian said nicely, "Please do ask her, Mrs. er—I'm sure we can lighten your load, and hers."

She breathed heavily and slowly to show how much thought she was giving the matter. At last she relented, and went back into the sitting room.

They waited. "I don't hear anything," Morris whispered.

His mother came out, with Bea supporting her like an invalid.

Morris felt an urge to shout, "Come on, Mom, stand up!" ashamed to see her so.

She said, "You knew he was coming here."

Morris grated his teeth and looked away.

"You knew, and what did you do? Played soldiers all evening."

103

"They're not soldiers."

"*All evening!*"

"Without so much as a phone call," Bea prompted.

Annie pushed away to step forward.

"He'd have come here anyway," Morris said. "He said he wanted to give us Christmas presents—oh—" his own were lying unopened at Patrick's—"he was having a fit of goodwill."

She sighed heavily.

Bea put in, "That's not how it looked from here; upsetting your mother."

"Kelly's listening on the stairs," Morris said.

Bea darted him a look of pure venom before she clattered upstairs. They all listened to her ungentle attention to her daughter. Now Morris felt he could breathe more freely.

"Mum," he said, "this is Ian." (*Don't mention Patrick.*) "He says I can go and stay—Ian, you tell her." He crossed his fingers behind his back.

All the while that Ian was explaining, like a salesman on a social call, Annie Nelson watched him as if he was speaking in visible subtitles. Only at the end, when she didn't respond, did Morris add, "Then you could do whatever you liked," and quickly shut up at her narrowed stare.

"Do what I like!" she echoed bitterly. "With *him* hanging around."

"If we'd only stayed at home," Morris muttered.

"Yes? What then?"

"Nothing." Thinking: *Then we could all have had our Christmas rows without making a public show.*

"But we didn't," she said. "All right. Blame me. Life's easy, with hindsight, as you'll doubtless discover for yourself."

"I know." It was so shameful, exposing all these sores in front of Ian, who was harmless and kind. Morris glanced at him, and he took up his cue.

He said, "I'm sorry, Mrs. Nelson; please think about it; Morris is very welcome to come to us."

She blinked, halfway out of a trance. "Thank you," she said, "you're very kind. You see—" and didn't want to tell him. She started again: "It did seem possible that I might have stayed on here, just by myself—" She looked up at Cousin Bea, drawn by danger into the arena. There was some attempt at a smile.

"Of course," Bea said a shade too warmly. "By yourself; but with that—*man*—with Matt turning up and so unpredictable—well—"

Both women stood up very straight: *Weapons at dawn*, thought Morris. *That rotten Bea's gone back on what she said and it's all wasted. Christmas a time for the family? Some sweet family she's got! Surely, now, we'll have to crawl back home.*

The silence seemed to go on for ever. It was everyone's and no one's move. At last Ian said, "If you like, Mrs. Nelson, you could both come, at least till you decide what you want to do."

They all stared at him. Mouths opened and shut without issue. Morris thought his mother was going to cry, which would be dreadful. Ian ought to sprout wings and a halo. "If you doubt it, I could ring now 105 and see what my mother says, before you decide any-thing."

"Strangers," Bea murmured, as one would say, lit-tle green Martians.

"One night?" Annie Nelson said.

"Whatever you like. I'm sure. Now, if you like."

"One night. And I don't know how to thank you."

"Rubbish."

"Can you wait? I'll just get—" She started up-stairs, to collect their belongings together. Astonished and mortally affronted, Bea rushed after her, telling her in an intended-to-be-heard voice how stupid this was, trusting to the word of a quite unknown young man, a *confederate* of worthless Patrick's, probably liv-ing in the same kind of squalor, with a fictitious mother who might well not allow them even over the doorstep—

"At least the son is making me welcome," Annie answered, just as loudly. Morris grinned at Ian, need-ing all the luck they could muster.

"And suppose they do take you in," Bea went on. "What'll you do when *that man* follows you there? He will, mark my words—if he's been to Patrick's al-ready, it won't take him long to find you out—that'll be nice, in a stranger's home!"

Morris's grin faded but Ian shook his head.

His mother called, "Morris, come and get your things!" He dashed upstairs, the sooner the better.

When they were ready, she answered Bea's last point, but to Ian. "Please don't worry," she told him. "There won't be any scenes in your house, I promise you. Besides, I think it best after all if we go back home; but one night in a civilized house would be so welcome."

If Morris's hands hadn't been full of luggage, he'd have hugged her.

12

As soon as they were introduced, Annie Nelson made it quite clear to Mrs. Comber, Ian's mother, that they would only be staying overnight. Tomorrow, they were going home. Morris felt too tired to make any of the remarks that came to his mind.

Quite soon, Ian went out again, to meet his girlfriend. Mrs. Comber said they were getting married next year. As Ian hadn't contradicted this, Morris supposed it must be possible to be a human being as well as a dedicated games-player. Or even a human being as well as a married man.

When he saw his and Ian's mother deep in self-contained conversation, he left them alone. He felt at the same time both hollow and over-filled with a terrible clutter of wretchedness.

| | | | | | | | | | | | |

Next morning first thing, Ian volunteered to take Morris over to East Lodge and bring him back when his mother was ready to leave. "One last skirmish at the castle," he said.

Because he didn't look too serious, no one could really object.

Once they were alone, Morris ventured to say to Ian that he didn't now want to go home, in spite of having protested so before. Ian said he was sorry, but made no further offer. The subject was dropped.

Not feeling cheerful, Morris looked up at Patrick's house as they drove up, and remarked on what a dreary place it was.

"I doubt he notices," Ian said.

"Does he always have setups, like the castle?"

"Always something—like or unlike."

"My mum said he did, since he was a kid."

"I can well believe it. Good luck to him."

"How long's he had this one?"

"Not so long. Part of it is constructed on a setup he had some while ago. Not the castle, that's new." He sighed. "I fear it won't last long, though."

"And the little figures—are they new?"

"Oh yes, they're an integral part of it. Fascinating really."

"That handbook—" Morris ventured. Ian waited. "Does it tell you how to play?"

"Not really, that's only a part of it. There's a whole load of background stuff."

"I wish I'd read that," Morris said wistfully.

"Yes, well . . ." He parked the car in the empty yard. They got out.

"Just think," Morris said, "we were going to stay *here*; we could have still been here, all the time."

"It's not exactly a woman's house," Ian said.   109

They went in. Patrick was in the kitchen, gulping

doorstep toast and reading some of his mysterious magazines. He and Ian started a conversation from the middle, as if they'd been talking for a good half hour. Morris asked, "Can I go upstairs?" and was waved on. *Oh, a few precious minutes alone with hope.*

The setup was in darkness. As he knew how to work the lights and hadn't been forbidden, he adjusted them to a nice cool morning, to give a fair view. Then he rushed down to the farm and lay flat on the floor to squint through the windows. There were a few figures in their beds, unwakened. None in any other rooms, none in any other buildings. His mouth was dry—Wait; hadn't Vail fooled him before, cleverly camouflaged somewhere outside—he adjusted his vision to scan walls and banks and the bridge over the water. He met no eyes waiting to key into his own.

The two bosses could be here any time. Morris took himself over to the forest side. The little Westgate was shut; the ivy, seen on this scale, looked as if it had never been disturbed. Hopeless: she'd gone in there, into the maw, leading her reluctant army, to be treated to that fate truly worse than death—and not resurrected.

A tiny movement on the ground among the trees pulled his eyes back. There, quite close by, was a little man, as shadowed as his surroundings, warily waving one arm. He was plainly bracing himself against not running away. When he knew he had Morris's attention, he put both hands together as Vail had done and waited for the great one to speak to him, or not.

Morris said softly, "I've seen you before. You came and gave Vail the key to that door."

"Yes, Lord."

"Where is she now?"

"Within, Lord." The young man clasped his hands tighter together.

"But you're outside, here? How come?"

"I'm West Village Kin, Lord; poison to that place."

"West Village?" Morris's eyes ran over the bumpy ground behind the young man that showed where the mythical village had been.

"The true and only descendant, unresurrected and bearing sin. I am descended from that one who was the only survivor of the innocents who went joyfully into the castle. The keybearer." He was both ashamed and proud.

"But she—Vail—she didn't believe in that old story," Morris said.

"She knew it was true," the young man said sadly.

"She told me otherwise," Morris insisted. "Surely she wouldn't have gone in there if she'd believed it'd be the end of her—and the rest, too."

"We have different fates, Lord. Hers was to achieve entrance and ingestion, by whatever means."

"Ingestion?" *Oh, nasty, gobble, gobble* ... Swallowing nausea, Morris said, "So why have you come to tell me this?"

"You knew it too," the young man said, "so now I'm at your service, Lord, if we're to proceed."

It was so stupid being called Lord without a clue as to what to say or do next. But too late to refute   111 the title, of course. At the back of Morris's mind floated the thought that he ought to get hold of the handbook. Now he was saved from floundering by the young man's producing the precious key from an inner pocket and holding it out for examination.

"Good," Morris said, "what will you do with it?"

"It's yours now," the young man said. "I can't penetrate further into the castle alone. I've been twice back into the Dancing Court since their passing, and as you know, they are all gone from there every one, and none resurrected. They've been treated just as my own ancestral kin, and that's not right." Then he seemed to recall who he was talking to, and lowered his eyes, respectfully offering the key at arm's length.

Can I really take it? Will it turn into a piece of dead merchandise in my hand, like the poor removed figures before? Unable to resist, Morris inserted his hand between the trees and took the tiny key carefully from the brave young man. It was less than the length of a pin, cold and metallic.

The young man said, "I shall be ready when you will, Lord."

Morris said, "All right, Sam; I'm calling you Sam."

"At your word." He seemed to melt into his surroundings. Too late, Morris thought to ask, How shall I find you? But Vail had always known what to do. There was something more reassuring about Sam: females in any guise were not comfortable.

Morris sat back on his heels and looked closely at the key. It was a fine little thing, with a complicated working end; strong too, though he didn't test it too much. It was like a charm from an antique grave.

The problem was, how to use it. Strictly forbidden to touch anything on the actual setup, Morris couldn't see how he was going to fit the key into its lock. Unless the time was come when Patrick was about to open up the castle as he'd threatened. Meanwhile, the key was put into a small empty pocket, zipped across for safety.

Ian and Patrick were coming up the stairs, still not agreeing on the castle's fate. If it was taken to pieces, Morris wondered, what would they really find? Maybe the hollow, working shell as Patrick had said, or maybe all the poor prisoners and the brave maid, their leader, suffering torment in vile dungeons. Whatever, it would have to be sooner than very soon if he was to witness any of it.

He looked hopefully at Patrick, who was slowly pacing the perimeter like a predatory animal.

Ian had turned to the handbook. "If we could find our way through all this mumbo jumbo," he said, "I'm sure we could set it to rights without destruction."

"Well, they shouldn't make their literature so hellish intellectual," Patrick declared. "And after buying the new additions, it's too bad. I haven't even unpacked them yet." He puffed a bit and added, "My festive treat to myself."

"What did you get?"

"Forget now; the stuff's still downstairs."

"Shall we see?"

"Well, what's the use—"

"Oh, come on," Ian said, "you could at least *see*: What did you get? What'll it do?"

113

"Told you, I forget. I can't be bothered with opening it all up now. Tomorrow'll do."

"But I won't be here tomorrow," Morris pleaded.

"No? Never mind. Help yourself." Patrick waved grandly. "I'll just go and check on those things." He left them.

Morris stared gloomily at the ever-triumphant castle. "What did he mean, 'help yourself'?" he asked Ian.

"I don't know. Do you want to try a last game, a shortish one?" Ian glanced at his watch.

Morris felt suddenly sulky. "It's all right for you—" a glance—"for him; throwing his money about, playing games all the time. Real people don't mean anything to him, do they. *Never mind*—of course I mind!"

Ian defended himself by looking through the handbook, as if it contained all the answers to all their problems. "A short foray?" he said hopefully. "Another sight of the castle defenders? They're usually worth it. Besides—" he illuminated the screen—"I think we're still well down in numbers on the guerrilla front. Something definitely went wrong there; they didn't re-form yet, you know." He flicked quickly through the farm buildings to check out the troops. "Castle United 10, Peasant Rovers 0." He glanced at Morris to see his response.

"All right," Morris said.

While Ian's back was turned, Morris felt in his pocket for the little key; that it was still there was quite surprising, though it could have puddled into a bit of useless plastic by now. He didn't dare look. He asked Ian, "When you said they hadn't re-formed, did you mean they hadn't remade themselves, like they usually do?"

"That's right. And you see, that's trouble, because if they took to not doing that all the time, we'd run out of attackers pretty soon, after which there'd be no point in the game at all."

"So what are we doing this time?"

"Lone snipers; it's all I dare risk till I know what Patrick wants to do. What a war!" He turned from the console, ready to begin, and pointed to the screen.

"Which view's that?" Morris asked.

"South Curtain Wall, below the battlements; where the sappers, now lost probably, tried to sink a mine, before. This little lot won't have much of a clue about that; never mind."

A party of three was standing as if undecided what to do, staring at the ground. One of them poked at it with a longbow. They didn't appear to be in any great hurry, considering Ian had called it a short foray.

Without thinking, Morris asked, "What kin are they?"

Ian looked sharpish at him. "Come again?"

"Nothing."

A silence while they watched the three figures slowly come to a decision and separate out to present three widely spaced targets.

"I felt bound to call on the Moorfold lot," Ian said. "We don't use them often but they're down as sharp-shooters."

He knew what I meant, thought Morris, *but kin was a*   115 *word I shouldn't have used. Perhaps it's in that handbook I'm not supposed to have seen. That I* haven't *seen. Better watch my tongue.*

As the three men took up their positions, each one ready to loose an arrow, one raised an arm for a signal, at which a high, long drawn out horn blast was sounded from somewhere behind and to one side of them. Ian adjusted the screen and pointed on it to a fourth figure, so well camouflaged that he could barely be seen, even in close-up. "A sort of Robin Hood," Morris murmured. That view bucketed away to be replaced by a scene on the castle wall, where a lookout was scanning the distance to discover what had challenged them. The picture zoomed in and for the first time Morris saw what one of the defenders really looked like. To his complete surprise, it was a girl, a young thing with long golden plaits tied with ribbons, a patterned blue and gold dress and a fine metallic cloak that glinted like tiny disks as she moved.

"Hey," he breathed, "she's all right; I didn't know they had girls on their side."

She turned and called to someone, who came up to her at once. This was a man, taller than she, bearded, also brightly dressed. He lifted his arm and a hawk took flight from his glove, with the far-off sound of tiny bells. The bird lifted high into the air and hovered. "Oh no," Morris cried, "it'll be shot!"

"No," Ian said, "they'll be wiser than that."

The hawk suddenly took off at great speed, straight across the path of the bowmen watching below. Yet no arrow pierced its side, no telltale movement disturbed the still landscape. Twice more it flew across their ground. Ian nudged Morris to watch the castle wall. Now the falconer and the girl had been joined by several others, men in armor, cloaked and hooded, and another woman, older and proud, a jeweled coronet on her dark head.

"Oh, they're beautiful," Morris said. Poor drab Vail had quite gone from his mind. They were closely watching the bird; then the young girl leaned over the battlements to scan the ground below. She spoke to the others, and one came to look where she pointed. The hawk had swooped very low more than once: the falconer whistled strangely and it returned to his wrist. Morris thought the girl clapped her hands with delight. Then several went to peer out and search for whoever had challenged them.

But although the hawk had flown so close to the three bowmen, none had betrayed their position. "Can you see them?" Ian asked Morris. At first he thought he could, and then wasn't sure.

"They're very clever," he admitted. He was one moment on one side and the next on the other.

Now a new figure joined those on the battlements: the trumpeter. He too issued a challenge, but it was answered from a different place. Several of the knights walked along to the nearest lookout tower, each of them stopping to scan the outside as they went. The young girl ran further along than the rest and disappeared, to come into view again at a narrow window lower down in the wall.

"Ah," Ian said. If he understood, Morris did not. What were the bowmen waiting for?

The girl leaned out of the casement. Her long plaits hung down, the ribbons fluttering. She seemed to see something, leaned out further, and called up to those above. Her clear voice was choked and cut off as an arrow sped true through her throat. At the same time two more arrows took the falconer and one of the knights. The bird bated and then flew into the air as the older woman screamed and ran along the battlements. The knights who were furthest away, not realizing what had happened, stood target still and were picked off by the following flight of deadly accurate arrows. The woman reappeared at the window to drag the girl back into the castle; those left alive on the wall moved rapidly out of sight. It was all over.

"Well," Ian said, "that wasn't so bad, was it?" He switched off the screen and other controls. "Pity Patrick missed it, he'd have liked that. A bit thin, but active."

Morris didn't know how he felt. He kept seeing that girl calling so excitedly, then dead with the arrow in her throat. She was—delightful, so alive, now so dead. But what tremendous shots the bowmen were, and how admirably they stayed still while the hawk was skimming their heads. Beauty and death, all the time.

"I'd better take you back now," Ian said.

Morris nodded. *That key: useless.*

"We'll see what Patrick's up to, you can tell him he shouldn't have missed it."

They went downstairs, one blink and back into the old dreary world again. (*It wasn't real, that girl dying; only a game.*)

Patrick was in the kitchen. He looked secretive about his festive treat, but pleased. Ian said, "I'm just taking Morris back."

Patrick came out of whatever world he was drifting in. "Oh," he said. "I forgot—your mother rang— she's calling round, you're to stay here till she comes."

Morris stared. "Here? But why? When?"

"Soon, she said. Cross my heart, no fooling, that's what the lady said; stay here till she comes."

"To fetch me?"

Patrick shrugged. "She'll tell you, no doubt. Meanwhile coffee's on."

Ian started to tell Patrick about the "short foray" and Morris was left to wonder alone.

13

Morris said, "Shall I go back upstairs?" but neither heard him.

Patrick was so odd, untouched by humankind and the involved dealings that turned people inside out. But he was never to be taken for granted; he was never safe. Morris supposed that Ian was his friend because of the setup. Ian thought about people, until Patrick's world took him over.

Morris went back to the room to see what had happened to the castle dead, especially the girl. The monitor screen was blank but that didn't matter. In the clear cold light he was perfectly able to see that all the dead had been removed. The battlements were deserted, the fatal window empty. But a little way back from that window, there was a figure looking out, only partly visible. And on the ground far below, a single bright ribbon.

Hearing voices on the stairs, Morris called to them to come and see. Ian was interested and at once brought the castle window into focus on the screen. "You're right, Morris," he said, "there is someone there—it's the queen-type woman from off the battlements, I think—see her crown?"

"Yes. Yes, it is her. She ran to the girl, didn't she; that was the window where the girl was shot."

They fell silent. The woman was gazing so sadly out across the plain, grieving; perhaps the girl's mother.

He didn't want to think about mothers. "There's one of the girl's ribbons on the ground at the foot of the wall," he pointed out to Ian.

"So there is. That's unusual, leaving something behind. In fact, I've never seen any of the castle inmates before, except during play—have you, Patrick?"

"No." But Patrick wasn't to be charmed. He'd missed the action and wasn't interested. "Let's have a slow pan along the top of the building, Ian; line it up with that ridge that sticks out just below the battlements. That's it. Now slowly along."

It seemed a very dull thing to linger over but Morris didn't dare ask what Patrick was looking for. Slowly, slowly along a stone ridge like a rim—ah yes, like the rim of a box. He was trying to find a way to open the box.

Twice Patrick told Ian to halt the camera; twice he looked carefully from screen to building, examining some almost invisible mark or projection which might prove a possible entry. But no; on again. All the while, Ian said nothing. Morris was certain he didn't want to force the castle in that way, but then, it wasn't his to play God with. . . . *They both called me Lord, Vail and Sam* . . . and Morris put a hand to his pocket to feel the slender outline of the secret key. Which was going to be of no use in any of the likely outcomes. It would have to be a sort of souvenir. What a come-down.

Having searched the length of one wall, Ian was now tracking along the next. Then the ridge ended in midwall, and he waited for instructions. Patrick swore under his breath and went round to the other side of the castle to see what the ridge did on that side. He swore again.

"There's no lifting it piecemeal that way," he said. "It's too bloody eccentric." He came back. "Can you get a view *on top* of the roof? Do a helicopter landing?"

Ian didn't think so.

"Why not?"

"It won't adjust for that. It'd have to be modified in some way, but at the moment I don't see how."

Patrick paced up and down, clasping and unclasping his hands. "That thing," he said, "was put together, so it can be taken apart."

"What about your Christmas treat?" Ian asked. "Aren't you going to try that first, whatever it is?"

"Hmm. It's only extra components; I don't know —let's have a good look round the north side."

There was something not right about the idea of slicing the roof off the castle. Since Morris didn't see himself being in at the kill, he was inclined to side with Ian. They were completely absorbed: he wandered casually down the forest side to sneak another look at the Westgate. His mother could be here at any time, a thought best stuffed away.

Standing, he could see the door as before. He got down on the floor and squinted through the trees. You wouldn't think that old door had ever been open. The lock and handle were quite covered by the spreading ivy. Morris took the tiny key from his pocket and looked at it. It was surely made of metal, not plastic. He told himself that if only Patrick and Ian were to leave the room now, he would climb over those trees and open that door, regardless of the consequences. He believed it, too, to such an extent that it was physically hard to stay still where he was, like having a dreadful need to shout out loud in school assembly, or start singing in the doctor's waiting room.

As had happened before, a small movement, a flutter, arrested his eye. A little figure, perfectly camouflaged, was sitting on the ground beneath a tree close to the path, watching the doorway.

Morris breathed, "Sam," and again, and the figure turned his head slowly, then stood up and came silently nearer.

Morris beckoned him even closer. He couldn't trust that Patrick's absorption was a hundred percent.

Sam came almost to the edge of his world. He stood there, breathing noticeably hard, not speaking. What would happen if he stepped over the boundary? Death and an old box-coffin. Morris put a finger to his lips, then showed Sam the key, between finger and thumb. Sam nodded, with a look of fearful concentration.

From out of another existence, Ian said to Patrick, "Your front doorbell's ringing."

Patrick said where it could go. Ian glanced at Morris and reminded Patrick that Morris was to be called for. Patrick said, "Just hold it there, I'll be right back," and rushed away. Morris was quite surprised that he hadn't been told to go and answer the door himself. He sat back on his heels, deliberately admiring the castle towers so that Ian wouldn't notice Sam, poor Sam, left quaking in his shoes on what must be his very abyss.

Ian said, "What were you looking at, down there?" Not threatening.

"The Westgate," Morris said. "It looks as if it's never been opened."

"That's it," Ian agreed, "this whole thing closes up on itself most cunningly. It's too cunning for Patrick, too slow."

"How will he get the top off?"

"Somehow, if that's what he decides to do."

"And then will he put it back on and carry on with the game?"

"Ah. He's very clever, you know. But this wasn't meant to be tampered with in that way; it'll resist, no doubt."

"How, resist? I don't know what you mean."

"No." Ian grinned oddly. "Neither do I."

From downstairs, Patrick called to Ian to come a minute. He made a face at Morris before he went. Oh, one minute in which to talk to Sam, to be wise and godlike for the very last time.

He began, "Sam, I have to tell you something. Important. Of the greatest importance."

"Honor, Lord."

"No, no—but listen carefully—it may be that I have to leave you. That terrible things will happen soon—do you understand?"

"Apocalypse? Ah, not yet, surely; the Five Terrors—"

"Oh, don't!" Morris cut in. "I know all about that" (a lie) "and I'm telling you, the time's at hand, so if you want to end your days believing all that stuff, you'd better start fitting it in double quick." Poor Sam's face was an open blank. "Now listen; are you in touch with all the other—with the others?"

"We are one mind, Lord, even I who have no kin." His face brightened. "By this I can be sure that the First Terror, of Mind Fragmentation, is not upon us. How then—"

Morris felt very like snatching him up and squeezing him. "All right," he said carefully, "so if you're in touch with them, I want you to let them know that a great disaster—you can say that if you don't like Apocalypse—is very imminent, so they'd better do whatever they can to save themselves."

Sam's face was blank again, then worried. "This is your Word?" he asked.

"Yes. Will you do that?"

"Honor, Lord; but what of the future?" Now Morris looked blank. "You have the key, yes; you will return to open all to us?"

"Yes," Morris lied.

"We rejoice." Sam smiled proudly, stepped softly backward, and melted into the forest.

Oh, it isn't easy, playing God; lies have to be told —rarely—to keep creation working. And all with the very best intention. It was quite thrilling really, imagining those little creatures getting their thick peasant heads together, discussing his edict—"what can it mean? what shall we do? where shall we hide?" all the hurry-scurry, fear, panic perhaps—what rubbish; they were a load of cleverly computerized games pieces whose "minds" were factory cloned to work together, activated by some distantly pre-set program to follow an invented race myth. . . .

There were people in the room, real people his own size, people he knew, who wouldn't call him Lord and account his every statement an honor. People to whom he was as much a pain and an interference as they were to him. Especially—oh save us, not only his mother but his father as well. Now fantasy leaps into every world!

They had funny expressive faces. They were going to say outrageous things.

"Hello, Morris," they both said, as if he was a long-lost relative or friend.

"Hello."

"Merry Christmas," his father added.

"You're still too early," Morris said. This was a ridiculous conversation.

"Not opened your presents yet, I see." And an unreal laugh.

"No," Morris said. "Santa Claus won't let me," playing along.

126   "Well," his father looked round the room with a

delighted smile, "that's all right, then; perhaps we can all open presents together; why not?"

Ignoring this silly remark, Morris asked his mother, "Am I to come now?"

But she also smiled. Morris began to wonder quite seriously if he was in the middle of a dream. "Not if you don't want to," she said.

"*No*," his father said quickly.

It must be a dream. "Do you mean I can stay for a bit?"

"Our friend Ian here," Mr. Nelson started (cheek, thought Morris), "has said, brave man, that he and his equally brave mother are willing to have you for a couple more days."

"Happy to have you," friend Ian corrected.

Morris studied the relevant faces, not knowing what to make of it. "But why?" he asked. "I thought Mum and me were going *home*."

"Wouldn't you like to stay?" she put in. "You were all for it a while ago."

Detecting a definite plea there, he asked, "But where are you going?"

She tried hard to appear casual. "Your dad and I thought of going to a hotel—just for a day or two, before—"

"*What!*" Morris gasped. "I don't believe it! A hotel, after all you said—Jesus, I just don't believe it."

"There's no need to swear," Mrs. Nelson said primly. "I'd have thought you'd welcome any chance—God knows how slender—honestly, Morris, I just don't know how to win with you. This isn't easy, you know." Her husband attempted to put an arm across her shoulders, which she resisted. "Nor am I promising any satisfactory outcome; but it's not for me to turn any possibility down."

Such grand big words; she must have been rehearsing them, polishing them up for this occasion. Morris looked up at the ceiling as a remedy for suddenly smarting eyes, for which he was ashamed. Again his mother glared meaningfully at his father: your turn. He stepped forward with that silly grin on his face and an outstretched hand to his obstinate son.

"Come on, Morris," he said, "this isn't the old Morris I used to know. Give it a chance, man. What do you say?"

All the old Morris could think of was: *It isn't fair*; hardly a strong argument. "I haven't had much chance to think about it," he said.

"True." They were doing their best to be reasonable. "We're only trying to work it out; only a couple of days, before Christmas; don't you want that?"

"Oh sure." Though Morris wasn't at all sure what he was agreeing to; peace at home, or a couple of days here. . . . It all seemed so ridiculous; how could months, years of family discord be set to rights in a couple of days in a hotel? (*And a couple of nights, Morris, don't forget the nights.*)

Forget it, be grateful for any offer. Think of the beautiful castle instead, controlled dreams, nothing sordid. . . .

Patrick suddenly came to life, to wind down the rather embarrassing scene. "Well, Annie," he said 128 cheerfully, "that's all settled then; nice seeing you, Matt; have a good time."

Annie blinked, not at all sure that all the necessaries had been said. Morris, she'd noticed, had shut himself off, as he had so many times before. "Morris," she said, "you'll be all right."

"Oh yes."

"We'll be back, and then—" It was a waste of time; his mind was patently elsewhere. But this was a very important juncture in their lives and not to be wasted. "Patrick," she appealed, "you will see Morris—" And could see that his mind was also apart from them. Sister and brother had never been close; appealing to him now was impossible. She turned to Matt, who was looking too longingly at the castle setup. Perhaps he too would rather play war than peace games. It must be time to go.

Ian went downstairs with them, making reassuring noises all the way. It felt very like, Annie thought, Morris's first day at school. The smiling teacher had said: He'll be fine as soon as you're gone, Mrs. Nelson; they always are. Of course it was true, it was what you wanted; but oh, how bereft, how empty it was letting go. Things never change.

14

Silence. Patrick, feeling that something ought to be said, volunteered the information: "Annie always was a mess."

Morris thought "mess" hardly the right word.

"Well, you know," Patrick explained, "she never could make up her mind exactly how she wanted to be—you'd be getting along with her like real mates for a while, then suddenly she'd change her mind and flounce off and you'd find yourself deep in solitary manure. If you know what I mean."

"Yes," Morris agreed, "I do know." He couldn't begin to imagine his mother and Patrick as children—though they'd been scarcely that, with Annie so much the elder and Patrick always the solitary games player. It was easier to identify with Patrick, even while he fended people off all the time. It was easy to envy him.

"However," Patrick said, "those old memory-lane trails are a waste of effort. There's enough to do here to keep us all busy. You can forget what they're up to for a bit."

"It's daft," Morris admitted, "being left here

was all I wanted; now it's not—oh, sorry, it will be, I'll get over it."

"Of course you will; I always did and we're the same family, after all." This closed the discussion.

Patrick went to the head of the stairs. "Ian!" he called. "Here a minute!"

Ian appeared and leaned against the doorway.

Patrick said, "That lad could do with a drink."

Ian said, "He's not the only one."

A quick survey over his setup, and Patrick added, "So do we all. Let's leave this little lot till tomorrow. I'm fed up with it."

Morris said, "You go, I'm happy to stay here and I won't meddle."

"Ah, get out of it," Patrick said, pushing him. "What's the good of sitting staring at this thing? It's like watching a stone growing." He went on pushing him, down the stairs.

"They mightn't serve me in a pub," Morris said.

"Who said anything about a pub? I've got enough here to see me through a stiff siege."

They went into the room with the shabby old armchairs, TV, and VCR. While Patrick fetched bottles and glasses, Ian sorted through a rack of video tapes and slotted one into the machine. Morris thought they might be going to watch a blue movie, well beyond surprise.

Patrick asked, "What do you drink?"

He shrugged. "Whatever you've got."

"Here, have this," Patrick said, offering a squat tumbler of whiskey, a good double.

Ian glanced up. "Put something with it?"

131

"It'll still taste foul," Patrick said. "Get it down in one go, Morris; do you more good. What're you putting on, Ian?"

The TV spat into life. Patrick sat back and groaned. No blue movie: the setup with the castle bathed in warm light, a scene from a fairy tale.

"Maybe we'll learn something," Ian said, "something we've missed that'd set it right without—"

Patrick murmured, "I doubt it," but watched all the same.

"When was this?" Morris asked. He'd taken a solid gulp of the whiskey and felt he'd better say something alert before any drifting off of the senses.

"September twenty-third," Ian said, "when it was still a novelty."

Patrick grunted. "When they knew their little peasant places and did as they were told," he said.

"But you've added bits since then," Ian reminded him. "The water and the bridge and that cottage or whatnot in the forest. Oh, and some extra forest, didn't you—" They were treated to a slow panorama of the landscape, then a gradually detailed view of the castle. The little band was playing and exercising along the high battlements, pennants flying. Down to the main doors, which swung slowly open, guarded by four stalwarts, armed at the ready. Four more came right out of the doorway, to pose kneeling, facing outward, ready to fire arrows, though there was nothing to fire at. Then out came a tall, commanding figure in full armor, a great sword in his hand, and behind him a young boy and girl with a pale hound on a leash. The boy walked the dog to the outer path and even onto the grass beyond. The girl bent to pick daisies and tall feathered grasses while all the men stood or knelt at guard.

Morris tried to say, "It's the same girl that was killed just now," feeling the words slide away from his tongue. With great care, he put the not quite empty tumbler on the floor and settled himself lower into the chair. He was glad that the room seemed to be getting darker and hoped no one would think to switch lights on.

The boy with the hound called something at the same time as it barked into the trees and strained at the leash. The sounds were thinly distant but very clear; the images were becoming uncomfortably fuzzy.

Patrick said, "Ah yes, I remember this; now it wakes up."

Suddenly, the dog pulled so hard at the leash that the boy let go. The dog bounded away into the trees and the boy ran after it, calling. The four kneeling men stood up; the tall figure plucked the girl back just as she was about to follow the boy; she called and yelled and kicked out, but the man handed her over to one of the soldiers, who bundled her back into the castle. At the head of the remaining men-at-arms, the tall man ran across the path, but had hardly reached the tree-fringe when there was a terrible scream and a clattering of birds. With no hesitation, the rescuers went to the sound—now the picture angled lower, tracking them through the trees, watching as two men were picked off before they reached the boy, and another two as they carried him back. Even at the gates, another took an arrow in the back, but two, and the leader, lugged the broken little body back into the safety of the castle. The doors were banged shut as several more arrows thudded into the wood.

"Bravo," Patrick cried.

"That's not the end," Ian said.

Morris tried again to focus on the screen, but it was very difficult. Sleep would be very nice. . . .

On the battlements above the main doors, the defenders were rapidly preparing to take revenge, called to muster by trumpet and drum. Again, the doors opened and a solitary figure was thrust outside.

Patrick chuckled, "Poor bastard."

At the part-open doorway appeared the mouth of an ancient cannon. A man-at-arms behind a huge shield poked at the cowering figure, who had no choice but to go forward. As he was shot from among the trees, the cannon blasted forth with a great belch of flame and smoke. As the attackers revealed themselves ("stupid," muttered Morris) they were in turn attacked from those behind the castle wall. There was a lot of shouting and it was all very brave but not at all organized. Morris's eyelids were so heavy that he let them fall. After that it was impossible to force them open. The hound. He wondered at the top of his head what had happened to the hound. A dirty traitor, running off like that. Put-up job.

Out of the darkness, someone spoke loudly into his
ear. With a superhuman effort, he made an appear-

ance of being awake. Patrick shouted, "You'd better eat something!" and then he swam away into the misty background. An uncouth sandwich had appeared on a plate by his side. He pulled himself up and started to chew: it didn't taste of anything and was very hard to swallow.

On the television, the same or another battle was in full spate. People were charging round and round the base of the castle walls, whooping. They came to a halt in front of a closed phalanx of fully armored troops, backs to the wall, and proceeded to slog it out, swords, cudgels, and fists.

Ian said, "We haven't sent the defenders outside for a long time now. Maybe that's what's taken some of the zest out of it."

Patrick grunted an answer.

The sandwich was awful; Morris let a wedge of it slip down between the seat and the side of the armchair, Patrick not being houseproud. Suddenly he woke himself with a snortlike snore, without realizing he'd dozed off again. The previous fight was over, replaced by yet more action. This was a real piece of medieval warfare, with boiling liquid being hurled down from the battlements onto the attackers below, to the accompaniment of a raving lot of sound effects. Things certainly had changed since whenever that was, both in scale and intent. You would have thought, looking at that scene, that the castle must either have been taken or the attackers all killed off, by now.

This time, Morris found he could keep his eyes

open with more success, though the sandwich was not sitting quietly in his stomach. He had no idea how long they'd been there, rerunning these scenes of past glory.

A battle ended, the many dead were carted off into the castle, the screen buzzed with empty patterns, another scenario began. This was a sort of gathering of the clans; a lot of peasants meeting together in their villages, preparing to march on the enemy. They carried pikes, bows, and arrows; they were dressed in their usual drab outfits but with added leather jerkins, helmets, and gloves, even an armored breastplate or two. As they were not quite ready to move off, the camera lingered from face to face, stolid and quiet, no signs of excitement or anger.

And there she was. Morris caught his breath and leaned forward despite himself. Vail, his first love (the mind still fogged with whiskey), standing among her kin, resting on a long pike and staring into space.

Patrick said brightly, "Oh, you back among the living again?"

Morris tried to grin knowingly.

"What's caught your eye?" Ian asked.

"Oh, nothing, just one of the model figures I—"

Ian touched a button and the film zipped backward, then started to replay; again the group of peasants, forming quietly into rank, one face and then another ... what did it matter, now? It wasn't possible to betray someone already ... ended. When Vail's face reappeared, Morris murmured, "That one; I remember her. . . ."

Ian held the picture on freeze. They all looked at her. Oh Jesus, such a gentle, honest face. Filling the TV screen like any face he'd ever seen, but twice as real. *I knew her, a victim, deceased.* How do you feel? *the interviewer always asks. I feel rotten, sick, and lonely, though partly due to drink.*

Ian said, "Was she the one taken out of the setup with the three blokes?"

"I think so." A very thick voice. He wished the film would run on again.

"Lovely face," Ian said. "It's marvelous, the high quality of the modeling."

Patrick said, "True, but there's only a few different faces—that doll there isn't the only one looks exactly like that."

Morris winced at the word "doll." Neither Vail nor any of her kin were dolls of any meaning. "Let her go," he murmured. Ian heard, looked askance, and moved the film on. Morris felt very tired, very heavy.

The lines re-formed, the peasant army (if you could call them that) began to stride in the direction of the castle. They showed a purpose, but already a brooding air of fate marked the way they moved.

"When . . . ?" Morris wondered.

"Beginning of this month," Ian said. So time had passed; time that was short to the gods but maybe a lifetime to the little people. Yes, as each one lost his life and was replaced, so it was, a lifetime. He didn't want to watch any more; he closed his eyes.

Patrick said, "You see, Ian, already the rot was set in though we didn't know it then."

Ian agreed. "I remember," he said, "we put it down to a poor choice of program. 'Next time,' we said, 'we'll liven them up.' "

They were silent. Morris dozed, hearing the tinny sound effects a long, long way away.

The show had ended. Patrick was walking about the room; the lights came on. "Come on, Morris, wakey, wakey," he said. "I didn't know you were a one-glass man." He laughed.

Morris found he was rather more awake, with an unpleasant mouth. "It's reaction to that family scene," he said.

"Ah. Well, you can forget that and enjoy yourself —isn't that what I said? You can sleep here if you like. My big sister Annie would never know. Or care."

"He'll be expected at home with me," Ian reminded Patrick.

"God, Ian," Patrick scoffed, "sometimes I think there's no hope for you. Poor old Morris, see how they wear him out—I know Annie used to wear me out when I was a kid; think of all the practice she's had since then."

Ian grinned but didn't answer.

"Well, what shall we do now?" Patrick went on. The earlier dumps seemed to be forgotten.

"No, I'm going now," Ian said. He glanced at Morris.

"Whatever for?" Patrick asked. Thunder threatened
to return.

"I do have other things to do."

Patrick groaned. "The girlfriend. I tell you, old thing, your days of freedom are well into the final countdown."

Ian looked quite calm at the prospect. "We'll have to see," he said.

"God help us." Patrick turned his back. "You can go hang for all I care."

Ian glanced at Morris.

"And he can go hang as well."

Ian sighed. "Come on, Morris." There was no choice.

"And don't bother to come back!" Patrick bawled after them.

"Does he mean that?" Morris asked Ian.

"Only for the time being. Come tomorrow, he'll have forgotten all about it." They let themselves out.

"Will he do anything to the castle before then?" Morris asked.

Ian shrugged. "Who knows. Probably not. Most likely thing, he'll have a good eat and drink and watch TV till it sends him to sleep." He paid the house a final glance before driving off.

It was very cold after the centrally heated house. Morris's head had cleared. He ventured, "Patrick must be a funny sort of friend."

"You get used to him."

"He frightens me a bit."

"Oh—" Ian paused as he waited to turn the car 139

into the main road. "Oh, there's no need. He'll take it out on the setup, not you."

Morris wasn't very sure about that. For example, he imagined Patrick would be wrathful if he knew about his dealings with the little figures. That secret key, which he knew he shouldn't have; the understanding with Sam—oh. How odd; he'd promised Sam he would return (not believing it at the time), and now it would come true. He wondered—"What is it Patrick's going to put into the setup tomorrow?"

"No idea," Ian said. "Could be anything."

"Shall we get to see?"

"If he hasn't gone berserk on the thing in the meantime."

"But you said—"

"Who knows?" They drove through the little town, where a band was playing carols and people were singing. All the fir trees above the shops were lit and all the windows were in the final stage of enticement.

Morris said, "Can you stop? I want to get something for your mother."

He remembered then the boxes of chocolates already bought for presents and forgotten.

Ian said, "You don't have to, she wouldn't expect it."

"No, really." The chocolates had been left at Cousin Bea's, as far as he knew, but not having an inventive mind, Morris now bought Ian's mother another, bigger box. He had enough money for a couple

of packs of sweets for Ian and Patrick. Thus ended

his Christmas list. *Surely*, he thought, in a kind of desperation, *I have more friends and relations than that?* He sat beside Ian for the rest of the short journey with nothing to say, none of the old feeling of anticipation that used to mean Christmas; with nothing but a kind of sad surprise.

15

Another morning. Ian told Morris, "I'm glad you're an early riser. I've got to go to work but I'll dump you over at East Lodge first if you like."

"Will Patrick be there?"

"On and off. I suppose he has to show an occasional face at work too, festive season or not."

"Will he want me there?"

"Oh yes."

"After yesterday?"

"Oh yes. You mustn't mind what he does with his own property. It does all belong to him, to do as he likes."

"It's all right," Morris promised, "it's just that I don't know how to take him. Sometimes he scares me a bit."

"Watch out!" Suddenly, there was Patrick's face, beaming and squash-nosed against the car window. Morris hadn't even realized they'd arrived. They got out and were greeted like long-lost brothers.

"What kept you?" Patrick asked. "I've been waiting all this time to open the new stuff. You can help carry it upstairs."

"I've got to be at work directly," Ian said. "Morris'll help you."

"Oh come on, a few minutes."

"Fifteen, no more," Ian conceded.

Patrick took them to the box store at once and loaded them with cartons. Morris wondered how Patrick could have resisted temptation until now.

He was handed a plain box, quite large but lightweight, with a serial number on the lid. He bounced it a little on the way upstairs, to see if the contents rattled, but they were too well packed.

It was an enormous relief to see the undisturbed setup, with the guilty thought: *If it's going to be vandalized, I want to be in at the kill.*

Patrick was like a great big kid with his boxes, as if they were all a complete surprise to him. He wouldn't let anyone else open them and made a show of deciding which to tackle first.

It was very disappointing once again: what looked like sections of a building or buildings, a paper with instructions. Even Patrick looked faintly let down; glanced at the paper but didn't disturb the pieces. He went on to the next, a small box, more sections with instructions. Seeing Patrick's lack of interest, Ian took up the first paper of instructions. He didn't look very encouraged either. He asked, "When did you order these?" but Patrick couldn't remember.

Next he opened the box Morris had carried up. He said, "Oh," and, "Well now," and brightened up a little. Beautifully packed, several new model figures,

143

with a second layer beneath, like a box of chocolates. Creamy colored peasants, male and female, with two large dogs, the same color.

"Nice animals," Ian said.

"Funny lot of people," Patrick added. He set the top layer down on the floor complete for them to look at.

"Children?" Ian wondered, "you've not had children before, have you?"

"It's what they sent." Patrick shrugged. "I suppose it's what I ordered; there'll be an invoice somewhere."

"Children—" Ian got up. "Must be in the handbook," he said, "some scenario or other—"

Patrick replaced the figure, none too gently. He glanced sideways at the castle, sizing it up, how to get inside.

"Nice animals," Ian said again. He was already flipping through the handbook with some desperation.

Another box was opened, another surprise to its owner. "Good lord," Patrick said, "here, look at this."

Ian leaned over to see, then knelt down and handed Morris the handbook. (He held it tight but didn't dare read inside.) "What?" Ian asked. Patrick carefully lifted something from the new box; they all stared at it. "What on earth is it?" Ian said.

"A monster on wheels," Morris answered.

"Insane," Patrick decided. "I'm damn sure I didn't order that." He passed the little thing to Morris. It was fairly like a neat dragon rampant, yes, on wheels. "Which side is this meant for?" he asked.

They didn't answer, examining something else

from the same box: a bigger variation of the dragon, also on wheels. "Perhaps," Ian suggested, "they're part of some completely different setup, sent by mistake. Did you check against the serial numbers when they arrived?"

Patrick made a face. He muttered about the invoice, and left them for a minute to find it. Morris peered into the abandoned box. There were several more wheeled creatures still unpacked. They reminded him of something he couldn't pin down, beautifully crafted models.

Each one, even the smallest, was finely carved, with detail picked out in red, black, and pale gold. The creatures' faces were benign; the largest had a godlike dignity. The carriages were hung with tinkling bells, and the wheels were patterned. The dragons, or whatever they were, were plainly not to be taken as real. There were imitation garlands which, Morris saw, would chain the smaller carriages to the large one, so that the whole thing could be drawn along the ground like a triumphal—something—

"Can I take these out of the box?" he asked. "I think they all fit together."

Patrick said, "Sure," without looking.

On the floor, it was quite big, and, when fitted together, most impressive; the Dragon God drawn by three attendant dragons, with two more at the rear. The garlands were rigid; the whole thing could be wheeled along with ease at the touch of a finger.

Ian said, "Why, it's beautiful! But what's it for? A thing like that can't be part of the peasant stock-in- 145 trade, but it's not—" He bent to examine the creatures' jaws. "It's not the cannon-type weapon I thought it might be." He looked up. "Patrick, have you got that invoice? What is this thing?"

"A mistake, probably," Patrick said gloomily, not having found any invoice. "Some kind of toy; too big for this setup, you wouldn't get it through the ruddy doors."

A light fizzed in Morris's mind. He rushed round to look at the North Doors. "But you would!" he shouted. "I bet you would! Look, help me—" He and Ian lifted the thing and replaced it carefully before the castle main gates. Then Ian laughed.

"Trojan horse?"

"That's it!" Morris cried. "I couldn't remember—"

Patrick was ready to scoff, but got down on hands and knees for the right eye level. "So how do the troops get inside it?" he asked. "Get it back here, let's have a good look."

Ian managed to return the thing without damaging any of the landscape. They sat around and stared at it on the floor, waiting for Patrick to make the great discovery. He ran sensitive fingers over each line of carving on the body of the large dragon. No secret trap door sprung open. "Just like that bloody castle," he muttered.

He unhooked the large model from the smaller ones, to pick it up for closer examination. "Lens," he said to himself, put down the model again, and rushed off to find one.

146   "What do you think, Morris?" Ian asked him.

Morris didn't know. "Could be wrong," he wondered.

Ian also ran an experimental finger along the carving, as Patrick had done. "It'd have to be a very cunning and tiny door catch to fool the eyes of—" He stopped and laughed. "Sometimes," he confessed jokingly, "I get to almost believing in those little people, as if they could really and actually think and act for themselves." He didn't look at Morris, either ashamed or hoping to catch Morris out in a similar admission.

So what. "Yes," Morris said, "so do I."

"Why not. If we're going to play elaborate games, we might as well believe in them."

"Yes."

They sat one on each side of the mysterious dragon carriage, and waited. Ian appeared to have forgotten about getting to work.

Patrick hurried back with a powerful hand lens. He applied it to the dragon's flanks, muttering prayers and curses. Finally, most unexpectedly, a notch between the creature's wings was shifted with his fingernail; the wings moved as if for flight, and a small section of back (not underbelly, as they'd supposed) slid neatly aside.

Patrick picked the thing up, turned it from side to side, inserted his hand to explore the cavity. "It's quite roomy," he said. "This stuff it's made of is thin but good and strong. How many little peasants could we fit in there, Ian?"

"*We* don't, do we?" Ian answered. "*They* do that part."

147

"Get us one of those new figures, will you, Morris," said Patrick. Morris took up the first one to hand.

Patrick made a face at it. "*Soldier* types, Morris, not kids; aren't there any?"

Morris didn't think so.

"In the other boxes?" Ian suggested.

"Possibly. Never mind. Let's just see." Patrick put the child into the dragon's cavity. "You could squash a fair number in like flat sardines, but not sitting up ready for battle. They couldn't stand up either, monster's the wrong shape."

"But they don't need many, do they?" Ian said. "A few's enough—once inside the gates, they hop out and let in the rest. Wasn't that the story?"

Patrick mumbled and shrugged.

"I wonder how they get down to the ground," Ian went on.

"Slide down those chain-garlands," Morris suggested.

"Very good!" Patrick removed the figure and slid the cavity door shut. "Right," he said, "let's get on with it then. I knew I'd sent for something worthwhile."

"Did you find that invoice?" Ian asked.

"Oh, screw that." He went to investigate the still unopened boxes, searching for the missing soldiers who were to man the baited trap. Morris put the dragon carriages together again. Meanwhile, Ian returned to the handbook and Patrick hung muttering over his new toys.

148   Ian said to him, "I can't find any reference to a Trojan horse in here."

"Of course not," Patrick said. "When did that stupid book ever present anything in terms an ordinary man could understand? There's no new soldiers here, anyway; I suppose the thing uses our everyday peasants."

"But you're a bit low on them since that last set got swallowed up," Ian pointed out. "What about the new box of figures?"

"Oh, I'll just tip them in, God knows what they're for." And Patrick took up the box of children and the two dogs.

Ian arrested his hand, to compare the serial number on the box with an index in the handbook. "They're not for the Farmstead," he said, as Patrick was about to place them there. "They're supposed to be a kin set for up in the moors."

"And where'd they live, up there?" Patrick asked.

"Aren't there sectional buildings in those other boxes?"

"Very likely, but I'm not bothering with all that nonsense. I tell you, Ian, this is the very last and final appearance of the Siege of Castle Doom, and after this it's curtains for the whole lot. So you—" he stepped (still with care) onto the landscape and placed the new little figures, one after the other, onto the ground outside one of the farm buildings—"so you lot can take your luck with whoever's left, and do your tiny best, for God, boss, and country." He paused only to admire the two dogs. "Nice animals," he said, and placed them with the figures. "Now," he turned to Ian, "where shall we plant the Trojan dragon?" He stepped back and considered. "You

149

reckon they'd haul the thing up for us if we left it way up—"

Ian said, "Look, I must go; it's yours, you do what you like."

"They've gotten so bloody lazy," Patrick said, "they'd probably leave it on the village green as a thing for the kids to climb over. You sure it's not in the handbook?"

"Sure. Though if you want to hang on till this evening, I can give it a closer read; you know how obscure the text can be."

Patrick muttered to himself. Then, "I'll program the assault for night," he decided. "Better have a good moon, otherwise we won't see anything. Start the Dragon thing halfway along the road up the east side, under cover of the castle wall. Surely the lazy bastards can get it to the gates from there."

"What about the men inside it?" Ian asked.

"Oh, that's their problem. If they can't work it out properly, I'll smash their silly heads in." Which seemed a fairly sure fate in any case. "Now then," he looked at his watch, "start action in half an hour— no, an hour, I'm getting hungry—start it in one hour's time. That'll do. Leave it as open as possible; what the hell, it's their last fling."

While Patrick set it up, Morris stood and watched how the group of new figures gradually took on the protective coloration of their background, changing from cream to mottled gray-green. The dogs were the same. He wished he knew how it was done. It was all so marvelous; how could Patrick be so scathing.

And probably so very, very expensive, too. Incredible, to have so much money you could just blow everything up as part of a game.

Ian finally moved away. "See you later," he said.

"Right. We can all leave them to it. Coming, Morris?"

"Do I have to?"

"Oh, come on." Patrick pushed Morris's shoulder. "You can come up and have a look between times, if you want. Special treat, though I doubt there'll be anything to see."

They all three went out and the door was closed.

remember now," Patrick said (a dusty bottle of wine in his hand), "that your mother, Morris, was married at Christmastime. That's why she'll have been so struck with this second-honeymoon idea. She always was sentimental." Morris said nothing. "Matt, your dad, now he's got a much more organized approach. Couldn't organize our Annie, though, could he."

Morris said, "He left us."

"Now he's come back."

"To *her*, not me."

"That's life."

"Is it?"

"Yes? No? Who knows? I'll bet they don't, though they'll be saying it's all for the best. And that ought to include you. Shouldn't it?"

"I suppose."

"Here, have some wine in Grandad's crystal glass. Hear that ring?" Patrick flicked the rim. "I'm doing you an honor, bringing these glasses out."

"Thanks."

"I tell you what, Morris," Patrick went on, "it's

much safer playing little god with that setup, even if I have to blow it to bits, than tangling even *once* with my family. You can take that as my philosophy of life, if you like."

"It's a bit drastic."

"But still safer, in the end."

Morris tried to change direction: "But I'm not wealthy, like you."

"Ha ha." Patrick topped up Morris's glass. "You don't need a lot of cash to keep to a philosophy."

Morris couldn't answer that.

"Why waste time and energy on useless occupations?" Patrick went on. He was enjoying himself. "For example—" he delved into the freezer—"You see this all-in-one turkey dinner? A few brief minutes in the old microwave and hey presto! Why slave over a hot oven for hours?" He smiled broadly. "So what would you like—turkey, chicken, roast beef and Yorkshire pudding? You name it."

Morris wondered how it could be dinnertime, without a shred of hunger. "Can I have mine later?" he asked.

"Be my guest. Have a chunk of gateau, keep the boozy head at bay."

"Just a few biscuits," Morris pleaded.

"Suit yourself. I know what it is; you want to get upstairs to spy on the little men. Well, go on, but you won't see anything, there's another half hour to go yet."

Patrick's use of the word "spy" reminded Morris of Kelly. He didn't care for it, used like this, but went upstairs just the same.

Half an hour. The very last chance to talk to Sam, perhaps, to find out what had happened to Vail, who was lost ... He felt very melancholy, but the wine had not the same effect as the whiskey.

The room was in darkness, as of a cold winter night. He knew it was winter because it was cold, and the ground was once more thinly covered with snow. No people there; children and dogs all taken shelter. Too dark to see in at the windows, no lights inside the rooms (were there ever?).

No figures on the road to the castle; the unattended Dragon Carriage still under the lee of the East Wall, now in deep shadow.

At the Main Gates, silence and sleep; no waiting attackers hidden behind boulders or trees.

The forest, empty and undisturbed above the print-less snow. Nothing to see, as Patrick the God had declared.

In the place opposite the Westgate, Morris lay on the ground and called, "Sam!" barely above a whisper, three times. He took the tiny key from his pocket and put it on the snow, just over the border, at the edge of the trees. Bait, to bring Sam out.

And if he doesn't come, shall I leave the key there? What use is it to me? You could go in there, Sam; rescue Vail, warn her at least. Tell her I sent you. The Apocalypse comes.

Your mother, said Patrick, was always sentimental. *How like her I am.*

A shadow seemed to pass slantwise between the trees to the left, coming forward. It materialized into

Sam, dressed in white or gray, shades that shifted as he moved.

He stood by the key, but didn't pick it up.

"Take it," Morris said, "use it, see what you can do."

"Is it time?" Sam asked.

"Yes, it's time."

He took the key, weighty in his pale hand. He said regretfully, "This will only take me into the Dancing Court. What then, Lord?"

"We'll get you into the castle."

Sam didn't ask who the "we" were, only: "Shall your spirit be with me?"

"Of course."

"Then I fear nothing."

"When you get into the castle itself," Morris said (and he believed it), "I want you to find Vail—and the others, of course, and warn them, the Apocalypse is coming."

"Vail . . ."

"The girl who—Farmhouse Kin, she led the others through the Westgate."

"Her spirit was yours."

Morris felt his face burn. "See if you can find her; them. They're still in there, aren't they, Sam?"

"It's true they're not resurrected." Sam looked uncomfortable. "I confess, their minds are lost to mine." He scuffed his foot defensively in the snow. "But it can't be the real Terror, Lord; I joined with the new kin as soon as they arrived."

"The new—"

"Moorfold Kin."

"Oh, the new ones, yes. Tell me about them."

Glad to be on another subject, Sam explained: "Oh, they're very hardy folk, younger than any other kin; quick and cunning. Cunning above all." His voice faltered again. "It is foretold, they are the beginning and end of all our labors." He passed the key from one hand to the other, weighing many things. "The Fourth Terror," he murmured.

Morris could barely hear him. "What did you say?"

"The Fourth Terror," Sam repeated. "The Hidden Child."

"What does that mean?" Morris cast his eyes among the trees, as if they might conceal one or more of the new children, poised ready to attack them.

"Lord," Sam pleaded, "you know, and test me further than I can answer. The Moorfold Kin bring their fate with them, as is well known, but are privileged to keep it from our minds till they're ready. The rest of us only wait." He stared at the key in his hands, then looked up in hope. "Do they know about this?" he asked, presenting the key.

"No," Morris decided. "That's our secret."

"Secret."

Morris could appreciate that a secret must be a novel idea to one whose mind was constantly linked to other minds. Then it came to him what the Moorfold Kin's fate might be. "Sam," he asked, "do you know about the Dragon Carriage?"

"No, Lord."

"It's parked round the other side of the castle," he

said. "It's a sort of Trojan horse thing." Sam concentrated, but shook his head.

"I don't see it," he said. "It must be a Moorfold thing."

"Yes," Morris agreed. "I'll tell you—it's a big sort of dragon, on wheels, hollow inside, for people to hide in; they'll leave it just outside the main gates and then when the castle lot take it in, the people hiding jump out and open the gates to let in all the others. In the dark, so they can attack from inside and take the castle once and for all. It's been done before, at a place called Troy. I think it worked."

Sam nodded. "I see. The Hidden Child."

"Very likely."

"It is time for me to go."

"Yes, it is."

He saluted. "Keep with me, Lord."

"Good luck, Sam."

He turned, and was again a shadow flitting away between the trees.

Oh, Morris thought, *if only I could keep with him. If I used the monitor—no, that would only take me as far as the horrible Dancing Court; besides, Patrick might get mad. If only, some way, some way....* Muddled, at the very back of his mind, was a notion that Sam, real as he seemed, was only a computerized games piece, yet somehow linked up to the other humanized games pieces. Therefore, could it not be possible for himself to be also linked up with the rest...? Morris was not naturally imaginative, accepting all his conversations with Sam and Vail as they happened: now he couldn't make the mental leap he desperately needed, or even imagine, beyond the conventional, what Sam could be doing.

One thing only; he did come to himself quickly enough to transfer his eyes to the little Westgate, rewarded by the sight of his brave young hero arriving there. Sam brushed the trailing ivy aside, inserted the key, and gently opened the door. Before he passed through, he half turned, looking up, and made a small, proud salute toward his Lord.

Morris said, "I'm with you, Sam." It was all he could do.

He waited a minute, listening for sounds of distress from the inner courtyard. Nothing. Only time now to go across and see what had happened to the Dragon Carriage. He got up, but glanced once more down at the half-open door.

A large dog was approaching in the shadow of the castle wall, with unhurried purpose. It reached the Westgate and entered the castle, just as if it was going home. Even in the semidark, Morris knew it for one of the dogs from the newly opened boxes.

| | | | | | | | | | |

It must be nearly time for the final act to begin.

The Dragon Carriage was drawn up before the main gates, innocent and splendid, its dimensions perfectly fashioned to pass it with care between the fully opened doors. The moonlight fretted the gilded tracery and outlined each creature's head, so that the small ones looked joyful and the great one solemn and benign.

Really, thought Morris, the castle lookouts would have seen it being hauled and left here. Then they'd leave it strictly alone. But if that happened Patrick would smash the whole thing without any delicacy, so he hoped the action would go forward as planned.

He tried to spy the figures that must be there, waiting to storm the castle. They were invisible. He wondered where the second new dog was, and how much time was left before the action.

Not very much. What to do with it? Nothing of any real use. The handbook—where was it? A quick look at it might make all the mysteries clear. He remembered where they'd left it before. Fair game, it was still there. Though the light was not good, Morris found the large pages readable after the first guilty minute or two. The print was large, as if straight from typewriter or word processor.

He skipped the early pages, technical stuff. Lists too, probably component parts, with reference numbers. Quite a few ticked off. Morris ran a hurried finger down the lists to find the Dragon Carriage. Of course, it wouldn't be called that. The most likely seemed to be Votive Offering DB 614 a–c. 49. Perhaps 49 referred to the handbook page number ... He began to leaf through the floppy pages to find it, but was arrested by the word "Apocalypse" on another page. He read:

STATEMENT. The *Apocalypse*. When all Knowledge shall be revealed.

It is believed by all kin without exception that their world will come to its end, its Apocalypse (so called) upon the fulfillment of certain conditions or prophesies. The Final Revelation can come about only in this way.

Oh, Morris thought, *I wonder does that mean it isn't possible to open up the castle and see what's inside—bringing their world to its end—unless he does certain things—fulfilling the conditions. That it can't be done by brute force, only by following the rules?* It made sense to Morris, another games player.

He read on:

The Castle Kin believe that their doom is spelled with the coming of the Resurrects within their walls; the revenge of those they had previously killed, now immortal and invincible. Then will follow only surrender and death.

Question: How is this confrontation to be achieved?

There was no answer on that page. Now Morris appreciated Patrick's impatience with the book: surely all the working clues were there somewhere, only thickly wrapped up and scattered through many dense pages. If only he had time to read it all. . . . Page 21:

DH11–19:   These free-ranging creatures are at the command of the gods, to be their eyes in all inner places otherwise hidden to their view.

160   In the list of components, Morris found that DH11–19 were remote-controlled micro-cameras

concealed in the heads of various domestic animals, packed separately or as part of other sets.

Of course: the two new dogs, to film *inside* the castle.

Page 15:

The peasants contain but few leaders. Theirs is an overwhelming corporate yearning for the Castle. It is their history, their religion, their future destiny. Any leader is a figure of romantic adventure, not a campaign genius.

Question: How can these leaders be identified and their talents best used?

Again, not answered. Now Morris began to see how the handbook worked: you waded through the swampy information and used the questions as pointers when programming an attack. Yes. So, if only he dared tell Patrick of his great discovery, they could get their heads together and work out—

At the sound of footsteps approaching, Morris stuffed the handbook back in the shadows. Perhaps later, he'd tell Patrick, not just now. He tried to look casually idle as Patrick appeared.

He noticed nothing, going straight to the monitor. "Ah," he observed, "I see our Trojan dragon's all set."

They both admired the beautiful detail on the dragon, seen on the screen several times larger than life. "You still can't see how it opens up," Morris said.

"Let's just hope it does, that's all." Patrick glanced at his watch. "Come on, time's up."

161

Suddenly the bells on each carriage started to ring, clear and piercing, very like the crystal glass. No one had touched them.

"A signal," Morris said. He was looking, not at the screen, but at the castle itself: as the bells continued to send out their eerie harmonics first one light, then several more, appeared at different windows.

"Oh yes," Patrick murmured, delighted, " 'Here I am, come and see.' "

More lights, and faces silhouetted against the flares, movement from one level to another as of people suddenly wakened to a great excitement. A group gathered on the battlements, torches held high, leaning out, arms pointing at the dubious gift outside the gates. ("Come on, come on," muttered Patrick.)

Again the lights traveled between the levels, now downward; at last one of the great doors was opened, a very little, and three people emerged to investigate. Each bore a weapon and a long shield, and they approached the Dragon Carriage with slow caution. ("You do right, little mates," said Patrick.)

As one, the bravest or silliest, went right up to it and dared to touch its flank, the bells' sound trembled and died. They could watch what was happening on the screen now. The man touching the Dragon was old, wrapped in a long cloak, his sword and shield not held protectively. Probably someone who wouldn't be missed if the thing bit his head off. He slowly ran his hand along its side, very much as Patrick had done, and with the same nonresult. One of 162 the other two spoke to him roughly, plainly telling him to investigate all around the thing. He walked slowly all around it, and peered at the smaller dragons. Finally, he patted one on its head.

Patrick and Morris both chuckled, like an audience at a film.

Still the other two weren't satisfied. They gestured the old man to have a close look down the great Dragon's throat, and stood prudently well back as he did so. He turned to them and shrugged. A mighty discussion took place, with much head-wagging and arm-waving. Morris also noticed that the watchers inside the castle were keeping a concentrated guard over all this. They probably expected the three men to be picked off at any time.

At last, all three walked around the assembled carriages, poking and exchanging comments. Then they stood in a line facing the castle gates. Each raised his arms wide, presenting three unguarded backs to any aimed weapons in the darkness. There was a long silence.

One of the two doors opened; a double file of armed men appeared, facing outward. A solitary figure walked between them, at which the first three stood back in deference to let him approach the Dragon alone.

He gazed up at it, ran his hand around its open mouth, and finally caressed its flank as if it were a favorite horse. Seen on the screen, his face, in the cold silver light, had a grave authority. Morris had seen him before, hawk on wrist, that time the girl was killed.

163

"Look how he loves the creature," Patrick said. "Now they'll wheel it in."

Yet it seemed the man couldn't make up his mind. He stepped up onto the carriage the better to examine the patterned dragon.

"Do you think he's suspicious?" Morris wondered. "Does it feel hollow to him? Do you think he can *hear* something, from inside?"

"Maybe. Come *on*, man." Patrick was getting impatient.

Morris looked away from the screen at a movement outside its vision. A large dog was loping out of the trees. It went up to the man and raised a front paw to touch his arm. The man laughed aloud and clapped his hands.

"See!" he said clearly, "here's Gaveral our hound that was lost, safe from the forest!" And he lifted the leash end trailing from the dog's studded collar, in proof.

All the people watching from inside the castle clapped and cheered. "It's a sign! A gift!" they cried.

The man walked the hound back to the gates, which were opened wide. The band, which had been assembled, struck up a hearty tune. Before the man passed through the gates with the hound, he turned and delivered an order to his men-at-arms. The three who had been sent out first positively strutted as they fussed round the object which could have brought them instant death. Slowly, carefully, the Dragon Carriage was hauled through the gates and out of

164

sight. The sounds of rejoicing from the crowd could still be heard after the gates were shut.

"Good old hound Gaveral," Patrick said.

But Morris knew it for the second new Moorfold dog. Now both were inside the castle, ready to film all the scenes of capture, death, and destruction.

17

There was a profound silence.

Patrick sighed. "End of Act One," he said. "Time in the interval for coffee or something stronger."

"I don't understand," Morris said. "Interval?"

"Time for the castle folks to go to bed, so the attackers can set about their treachery. Nothing overlooked—we hope. Coming?"

"I'll stay here," Morris said. A thought: "Can I try the monitor again?"

"Help yourself. As long as you don't—you know."

How to home in on one of the dog remote cameras? Not much time for fooling about. Perhaps the handbook—no time. He tried to be calm, to read and assess each picture as it appeared on the screen. Repeated views of the castle walls, plainly the wrong sequence. He tried a previously untried knob, minutely adjusted. The screen went dark, but not blank. Morris paused, held the picture. Onto the darkness he saw, unclear, a picture of a room—no, a corridor, dimly lit. It twisted back on itself and the floor level dropped unevenly. The ground was dirt, sparsely flagged. The lights were thin, yellow shot with pale blue. The walls were stone and rubble. It was very strange; moving, traveling slowly all the time, a walking gait. Surely one of the two dogs, filming deep inside the castle . . .

Through an archway, also lit. Beyond that a wider, vaultlike place with arches; very damp. *Now I'm standing still, looking for—there! At the far end, the figure I'm following, a man hurrying but lost, searching for something.*

My God, it's Sam! I'm following Sam, I'm moving on again, padding in the dark, scenting his trail, loping. Loping.

Between the vaulted arches, no sound, out at the far side. Steps down, curving round, not easy for a large dog; have to hang back in case he hears the click of claws on the treacherous stone.

At the base of the stairs another corridor, very confined, curving to both left and right. Sam is out of sight, but his fresh footprints along the muddy floor point this way. There are other footprints here too, but none so fresh as to sustain the faint aura of light. Left. Where are we now? Below ground for sure.

If only, Morris yearned, *I could let Sam know I'm still with him; brave old Sam, searching faithfully for my Vail, my love. . . .*

The corridor straightens. There are decrepit doors in either wall; we must be going into the castle's very belly.

Where do these doors lead? We don't stop to find out, because the footprints go on. No sounds here; whatever the doors hide it isn't prisoners in agony or begging for life.

Now he stops and passes through a door, following the trail. Tiny room after airless room, door opening to door, like pulsing panic in a dream.

And suddenly a large room, low-ceilinged, low-lit; scented with cold and intense sorrow. We stop, because Sam is in view; he is bent over, looking at something on the ground. He lifts it to the light; a piece of torn cloth, almost transparent, perhaps from Vail's clothing.

Sam looks up at a series of muffled sounds from above, then tucks the piece of cloth into his belt and moves on, never glancing back.

"Hello," Patrick said suddenly, "shove over then, let's be at it."

Morris's fingers jerked the delicate tuning so that the picture was lost. Patrick seemed not to have noticed; to him the screen looked blank.

"Time's up," he said. "Let's be seeing Act Two. If we can. Could do with Ian to work this thing; he's better—oh well, here we go."

They were back again outside the main gates.

"Yes," Patrick commented, "they've just opened one of the gates, and not a sound." Two children, hand in hand, were ambling down the roadway to the trees. Then they separated and waved cheerfully to left and right.

He held them in focus on the screen. "Identical twins, from the new box," he said.

Gradually, without hurry, the two children were joined by more and more shadowy figures. Patrick began to hum tunelessly to show his approval.

The two children had the sort of coarsely innocent faces that Morris didn't trust in real life. He'd met their like before, trouble all the way. He didn't like them now. He wasn't at all sure whose side he was on: the castle people showed a brave dignity that the peasants lacked, but Sam and Vail were peasants too. (*The mysterious "leaders" of the handbook?*)

As the attackers streamed in silence up to and through the half-open gate, Patrick began to complain again: "What's the use if all the action happens *in there?*"

Morris thought, he must surely know about the remote cameras, seeing he must have ordered them in the first place. If not, it was a secret worth keeping to himself for a while longer.

As Patrick fidgeted randomly with the monitor controls, he lost the picture completely. "Goddamn," he complained, "all that action must be on by now in there, and I can't bloody get it!" He didn't have Ian's patience.

"There!" Morris cried, as something new appeared.

"Well," Patrick muttered, "it's something, but what—" He stood a little way back from the screen, squinting, to make it out. The quality of the picture was very like that before, in the Dancing Court, fuzzy and gray, with lines waving across the screen in irregular patterns.

"That thing, that dark blob down at the right-hand side," Morris said, "if you half close your eyes, doesn't it look like one of the wheels of the large carriage? The pattern on the rim and the spokes?"

"Yes, could be." Patrick tried to sharpen the picture once more, with a fractional improvement. "I think you're right. And that growing out of it must be one of the dragon's front legs."

"And you can see a bit of one of the garlands roping it to the other carriages."

Patrick grunted.

Something moved, first behind the static object, then to one side of it; something alive stooped to the ground. Then suddenly the picture brightened and became clear, though the angle was not the same. They could see the front of the carriage, a wheel and part of a garland, even one of the gilded bells that had so wickedly tempted the castle people to their doom.

"It's a weird view," Patrick said. "What was that?" as something rushed past in the background. He tried all he knew but the picture stayed obstinately static. He swore under his breath while they stared at the puzzle.

Morris thought, that could be the camera on the other dog filming now, the one they took in as the lost hound Gaveral. It seemed so likely that he thought he'd have to tell Patrick in a minute.

With a sudden swoop, the picture changed, so that they now looked straight across the courtyard to the inner wall of the castle itself. The backs of several huddled figures could just be made out through the dark. Then, as if an eye blinked to a higher power, the picture became clear, but oddly miscolored—probably infrared.

What were they doing? Three of those new children were tampering with a door, unaware or uncaring of the eye upon them. They successfully picked the lock but didn't enter. While two scampered off out of vision, the third kept guard by sitting on the ground, back to the wall. His face bore an odd smile and his eyes were constantly on the watch.

The watching eye left him, lunged again to one side, to catch one of the other two boys, who had rounded up a trio of peasants with nothing to do and was herding them toward the open door. They didn't appear very willing to go through there.

A rapid swoop showed a second group about to do the same.

The false hound Gaveral, Morris thought, *is filming all that's happening in this courtyard. The swoops occur when he turns his camera-eyes so as not to miss anything.*

After the two groups of peasants had disappeared through the door, with one only of the three children, the watching eye, finding no further action, lurched and moved toward the same door. There was a long pause while the eye gave itself time to penetrate the thick darkness, the picture gradually taking vague shape; an empty room, unlit, unpromising. Then it changed suddenly; they were moving again, at a lope, in the shadows, around a corner. They must be following the inner castle wall, searching for something. The place seemed deserted. Through an archway, then up stone steps, perhaps to the battlements.

Morris pictured the great hound questing up the uneven steps and wondered why the castle people 171 had let him go when they'd been so overjoyed to recover him. Were they already vanquished and slain?

But the hound wasn't making for the battlements after all. At a level probably halfway up, he turned aside and nosed at an unfastened door. He knew where to go, emerging into a well-lit place, at which the color switched back to the bright-realistic.

"Look at that," Patrick said. "So the castle isn't an empty shell—my God, to think I've never seen this till now."

They were high up, looking down on a vast space where people were grouped round a long table, drinking and talking.

"The detail's good," Patrick grudgingly admitted.

Several faces were turned up toward the viewer. They looked glad to see their visitor, pointing and straining upward and calling in delighted, tinny voices.

One left the table to stand alone and shout; the sound echoed from wall to far-off wall.

"What's he say?"

"Gaveral," Morris said, "the dog they'd lost and were supposed to have found again."

Patrick spared Morris a quick, sideways glance. "How'd you know that?"

It had to come out at last. "The dog's the cameraman; he's been filming all the time he moves around. The lenses are in his head, his eyes. . . ."

Patrick frowned, considered both Morris and the
172 screen, on which the picture dipped and jogged as the

treacherous hound slipped down to his master, who spoke:

"Where did you go, old Gaveral? Come, sit now, be still."

The image leaped suddenly to survey laughing faces and hands outstretched to stroke and admire.

"He's jumped on the table," Morris suggested.

"There were two dogs in that new pack," Patrick said. "So where's the other?"

Morris shrugged as if he didn't know. The other dog was different, special, working for him, searching for his own dear Vail. With sudden distress he thought in clear words: *All the people I love are taken away from me.* It shocked him, and he forced his attention back to the screen.

The people round the table were discussing what to do about the Dragon Carriage. They called it "the Great Offering." They were not all delighted with it and wanted to call for some kind of vote.

Patrick said: "That's not very medieval, voting. That Lord of the Manor bloke wants to put his foot down. He was lordly enough out there; all that rubbish about the lost hound."

A voice unseen said, "I maintain it's a secret weapon—and how many men do we have guarding it?"

"It's no weapon," the first declared. "It needs no guarding, Highborn."

"It needs to be watched," Highborn insisted, "if necessary, from the safety of a window. I don't trust it; we waste time."

173

"That's the canniest of the bunch," Patrick muttered. "Pity we can't see his face."

On cue, the hound swung its head to gaze at a middle-aged, bearded man, very like his lord, but fairhaired, one side of his face scarred from forehead to chin.

"A fighter," Patrick said. "I remember those two clones from the original starter pack. Twins, bosses."

Meanwhile the rest were having their say, with no decisions.

Patrick began to fidget again. "The way they muck about with the program," he complained, "they'll take all night over it. I'm damn sure all this wasn't written in."

With an abrupt swoop, the picture returned to the high gallery. Ringed round the wall, shadowy against the shifting shadows, was a line, one or two deep, of invaders, silently observing the debate below. Now the hound watched, slowly panning from one face to the next.

He jumped down from the table. His master bade him settle and stretched a casual hand to the massive head. The discussion went on and on. A vote was imminent. No one but Gaveral, it seemed, had noticed the silent invasion.

The hound padded to the foot of the stairs and looked up at the crowded gallery. One or two pairs of eyes returned his gaze, but most were fixed on the unwary talkers.

"Very well!" the lord cried, displeased. "We shall
174 mount a guard over the Great Offering. Nothing

more! Highborn, my brother, call your guard. I am going to keep my own private vigil in the chapel, that your hearts may be cleansed. Gaveral, Gaveral, come to me!"

But the dog stood alone in the center of the vast floor, staring up at the ominous shadows as they materialized into the light.

18

"The Resurrected are come!"

The people cried out; they drew in close together. The lord was unprotected. "Gaveral!" he called. "Come to me!"

The hound observed his proud stance but made no move toward him. Unarmed, he let his long cloak fall from his shoulders and held his hands palm upward as a sign of peace. Those distanced behind him froze in unfocused horror, with none of the brave show of the invincible. Only one rallied to his side, his brother Highborn, but he bore a sword in his left hand and his right arm guarded his brother's shoulders. Together they gazed upward at the shadowy ring of faces. If either were afraid, he didn't show it.

Behind them, a scuffle broke out as one ignoble soul broke for cover and ran from the hall.

"*That's* not wise," a young voice said.

A brief wait and there came a scream from the lower darkness.

"You see?"

"Who are you?" the lord asked.

"Your people know."

"You're no Resurrect!" Highborn cried.

"You know better?"

"Come down from there and show yourself," Highborn demanded.

"Unprotected?"

"Yes—if you really are a Resurrect, you'll know we can't touch you. Come near!"

"If I come—" the clear voice was moving along the gallery—"my friends come too."

There was a muttering behind the two men, a warning of danger from all quarters. The scream still echoed in their ears.

"I think," the lord said to the voice, "that whether we call you down or not, your friends are invading our peace. Am I right?"

"Peace!" The word darted from mouth to mouth along the high gallery like a hissing flame. The young voice laughed.

"We are here," it said. "We enter in your eyes, ears, nostrils, mouths; your ancient days are over. We are everywhere. The only place for your sword, Ugly Face, is in your own guts. See, I come!"

As the false hound turned to watch, the boy came slowly, insolently down the stairs toward them. He tossed a little gilded bell from hand to hand that chimed to remind them of their foolish fate.

"Where did you get that bell?" the lord asked gently.

"A gift from another friend," the boy said. "He waits outside. Perhaps I'll give it back to him, as he's such a good beast."

"How did you get in here?" Highborn demanded.

"Oh, my good friend carried me." The boy grinned and stroked the bell to make it whine.

"Stop your silly talk; answer my question!"

"Oh but I did, *Sir*. My friend the Dragon—" he shook the little bell—"he carried me, in his empty belly. And not only me, don't you think it!"

A sharp breath from the two men caused great delight to the boy. He snapped his fingers as a sign to the shadows in the gallery to advance. Then he laughed and pointed a finger at the cowering crowd behind the leaders. "You're brave," he said, "but your crew aren't worth spitting on. Look at them!" he told his shadows. "Can you believe, these are the very ogres you've been fighting fear against all your lives!"

Certainly the peasant crowd coming down the stairs showed much wariness. To attack outside, on home territory, was one thing, but parading in the enemy's house was entirely another.

The boy saw it, and found it hard to keep his broad face smiling. He addressed the hound in his path: "You, get off my way; there's more work for you than staring about here—go lift your skinny leg somewhere else—go find out the ladies, tell them we're coming!"

At once, so obediently, the dog took itself off to the far end of the hall, turning once to the lord, who returned his gaze with puzzled sorrow. The dog retired to the semidarkness at the edge of the hall, where it faced about to observe—to film—once more. More than one of the huddled people by the

table cast fearful glances in its direction, not knowing

what was waiting to attack them from just outside this room. And still the two brothers stood alone, confronting the boy and his engulfing friends. One of the people cried, "Come back here to us!" but the leaders took no notice. Now, the boy stood almost face to face with them, and the nearest of the shadows had reached the ground. Gradually, in silence, they fanned out all around their victims. As they did so, they changed from shadows to pale, mottled figures, flickering as they moved, like the lights in the hall.

The boy looked past the two men at the others, but didn't dare walk by. He said to his friends, "Ring them round! Leave no spaces!" and it was done. "Now, turn about," he ordered the brothers. "Look at your brave people."

They did so. "My Lord," one cried in anguish, "what can we do?"

"Stand to your full height," the lord answered, "die in glory."

Again the boy laughed; then he lifted the gilded bell, turning it in his hand for the right grip. With a sudden flick he sent it spinning at great speed across the room. Its razor edge severed a man's neck: he fell without a sound.

"There!" the boy called to his friends, "you see how easy it is! Kill them all! Leave only these two; their time comes after!"

The peasants were not as speedy as he wished; still something stopped them, a slow-motion reluctance to kill in this place, in this way. Angrily, the boy danced up behind one of the peasants, snatched his knife from 179 him and plunged it fiercely into his left side. "I shall call my true friends!" he shrieked. "Now kill! kill!"

The hound in the shadows watched, quite still, as all the castle people in the hall were slaughtered. None, with the eyes of their leaders upon them, made a sound as they died. It was not glorious or exciting, even to the peasants, who had waited so long for this moment. Neither the lord nor his brother Highborn looked away.

"Now," the boy said, "we must find what else is happening in this nasty place." He turned to the two men. "We aren't the only ones to have entered in," he said. "I daresay all your other folk lie like these, by now. But you are coming with us to have a look. You might be the last to die, or we might let your ladies have that privilege. Now you walk with us!"

Hearing those words, the hound backed slowly away, then left the hall, sparing a second's glance at a single body just outside as it passed. There were no alien shadows out here; whoever had killed that one had gone somewhere else, and too long ago for a trail to be shining on the ground.

The dog knew where to go. Along a narrow corridor, through a curtain, another, smaller hall, up a flight of stairs and into another corridor. Here there were several doors, all opened, probably by searchers: the hound ignored them all. At the blind end of the passage he nosed the ground until, right against the wall (where it wouldn't be trodden on), he found the ridge he'd been seeking, which sprung open a narrow trapdoor.

He peered through and down. The trap, on a time switch, closed after him. He stayed still until his eyes took on their highest power in the intense darkness, but even so, all the images were a purple blur.

On the ground, the ghosts of little footprints glimmered, pointing the way to a solid wall and disappearing beneath it.

The hound was not deceived by solid stone. Fingerprint auras flickering on one of the stones betrayed where fevered hands had pressed open the final secret door. It was no problem for him: the false section of wall, a tiny square, parted to reveal the last hiding place, the room that no pursuer should ever have found.

It was completely unfurnished but for a thick pile carpet muffling the floor. In the middle of the carpet, a hooded lamp cast its light away from the broken wall upon the five white faces turned toward the hound. All women.

One started forward in welcome, crying, "Gaveral!" but other hands drew her back.

"Who's with him?" one asked.

"Who *sent* him?" another whispered.

As he stepped into the room, they all moved closer together, holding hands: an old woman, two wearing coronets, one plain and middle-aged, one young and slightly apart from the rest, perhaps a servant. Vail? Morris almost cried out. If only she'd turn to face the dog. The old woman sighed and, passing the dog, not acknowledging him, peered out through the gap in the wall.

"There's no one with him," she said. She closed the tiny door.

"But why has he come? How did he know where we were?"

"He may have been followed, even as far as the trapdoor above."

"Have you betrayed us, Gaveral?" One of the crowned ladies took his muzzle in both hands to look into his eyes. Such a sad face, once and still beautiful. "What could you tell us?" she said. "You must have a mind, but it's closed to me. Are they safe? Or all dead? How long must we stay hidden here?" She fondled the hound's ears, then turned away, taking her sister's hand.

"Shall we leave?" this one asked. "Is there any point in this?"

"If they die, why should we live. . . ."

"I'll go up," the old lady declared. "I have no value. I'll find out for you and come back if I can."

"No."

"She should go." They all looked at the young girl (*Vail!*), who hadn't spoken at all.

"Of course. But . . ."

"Would she . . . ?" They seemed puzzled, as if they weren't at all sure who the girl was or why she was with them.

"I'll go if you want me to," she said. "You must tell me what to do."

"Find out what's happened, if it's safe for us to come out. Didn't you know that?" The old lady went up to the girl and gazed at her, very much as she had gazed at the dog.

The girl nodded. She said, "I'm not certain of the way back here."

"She wants us to open our minds," one of the other women said quickly. "We can't do that, we daren't, there's betrayal on all sides."

"I'll find you," the girl said, without threat. "Let me by."

"She could take Gaveral . . ."

"No!"

The square in the wall opened and she climbed out. The women regarded the dog, and he watched them.

19

They were staring at a blank screen.

Patrick said, "That damn dog's gone to sleep." He made to thump the monitor, and thought better of it. "You were right about the remote camera," he admitted. "I remember ordering them now. Two of them. So where's the other?"

Morris couldn't bear it and went to stand apart. The dog could sleep for as long as it liked: there was nothing in that airless room that he wanted to see. Dazed, he stood and yearned at the castle. *Where is my Vail now? What is she doing with the castle nobility? They didn't know how to treat her; they didn't know her as one of their own.*

Oh, but I did, Vail; I did.

Where are you now? Not dead. Not so.

The night was visibly lifting from the landscape. Cold, colorless dawn, a day to bring heavy snow. Time outside this place did not exist. *Oh, I wish I knew where she had gone.* The sight of her in that last hiding place had been such a shock he had almost cried out. *Don't destroy her now!*

Patrick suddenly made up his mind and brushed past Morris, almost knocking him onto the setup. "It's hopeless," he said. "Have to get Ian onto this, he'll know how to get it all working. Going to give him a ring."

"Isn't he . . . ?" Morris couldn't remember why Ian wasn't with them, where he was.

"This is *priority*," Patrick shouted as he clattered down the stairs.

Morris stared at the setup, in his head an image of Vail in that trap of a secret room, not being trusted by the castle ladies; an image of her gentle face, eyes looking at him at his own height, knowing him.

As the word "romantic" struck into his mind, he fled from it, to call after Patrick, who by now was on his way back.

He pushed past Morris and stood over the console, arms and fingers waving like a demented marionette, crying, "This one? or this one? What'd he mean, the left-hand side? facing which way?"

"What are you doing?" Morris asked.

"Got to go out, fetch old Ian; got to freeze the whole works till we get back."

"Stop the program? Can you do that?"

"Old Ian knows. He said—" Patrick made a decision which knobs and buttons to manipulate. He sighed deeply and cast a final long look of love and revenge on his doomed castle.

"Not long now," he said. "Keep an eye open, Morris. I'll be back. *Then* we'll turn it inside out!"

Morris heard the house door distantly slam. He 185

thought he heard a car starting up, or maybe not. He stood with eyes fixed on the blank screen for a rigid count of three hundred. It should have been five hundred, but he couldn't bear it any longer.

He turned back to the setup.

It was daylight over the landscape, and snow had fallen. No sun shone to beautify this world. It felt deathly cold, with the gray of deep depression. Forcing himself to move slowly, Morris looked first at the farmstead, once her home. Now there were torn gaps and crumbling walls, from no apparent cause. There would seem to be no one about. The place was desolate, as if it had been left to molder for many years.

He walked up and along the outside of the forest. In one section there was a cleared space, with the long-dead trees left as they'd been felled. Where the abandoned village had been, the ruined buildings were rising, like mossy teeth, through the ground.

The little Westgate was open, yet barred by a dense curtain of snow-covered creeper. An immense time must have passed. Morris felt like an unwelcome ghost. How could this have happened so quickly? Had Patrick followed Ian's instructions all wrong? If so, it would be no use looking for Sam, who would be long dead. And those poor women shut up in the secret room would be clean skeletons by now. *And Vail, too. My little love.*

He felt himself blush, but with no one to scoff it didn't matter. He thought again: *Vail, my love.* It made him smile, and then sniff, to have found and lost her in the many years that were really only minutes.

He went back to the monitor screen, just in case. It was quite blank. Knowing how to work the video controls, he ran the tape back a little and then set it to play. No response. He ran it back further and tried again. This time he was rewarded with some sort of picture, though faint. He let it play, but could make nothing of it. He rewound the tape even further and started to play it over from there.

Yes. The women in the secret room. Not moving, a set of dolls in a tableau. Only one was looking directly to camera (the hound); the rest were either asleep or dead. They went on doing this for so long that Morris reached out to run the tape on; but then the one looking (she was wearing a coronet) moved. She got up from the floor and came with great care toward the viewer, her eyes fixed and staring. There was no way of knowing how long they'd been there or what had happened to the others: they made no movement at all; only this one showed any life.

The hound made no attempt to stop her as she passed him. He followed her with his eyes; she opened the square in the wall and climbed out, as if it was causing her pain. She went laboriously up the stairs and waited, knowing the trap door would open for her. Then she was out into the castle itself, never once turning around, though she must have known she was being followed.

Perhaps now, thought Morris, *I shall find out what happened to the rest of the people.* His heart seemed to be beating in his throat.

The woman walked very slowly, and the hound 187

trailed her dragging skirts. Three times, she stopped and bent to a still figure on the ground, then passed on. The hound took no interest in anything she found.

She came to the great hall, where there were more bodies, which she examined. He waited until she was done, and then, oddly, she turned round to him with a long look of grief before walking on.

They came out into the courtyard. It was daylight there, but snowless. The woman drifted up to the Dragon Carriage, standing in abandoned glory. Here too were more bodies, which she stepped over to approach and finally touch the creature itself. The hound kept well back to observe all she did. She gazed up at the treacherous thing, her hands on its flank, perhaps trying to understand their fate. Then she let her head fall onto her arm, as if she were weeping.

When the hound went closer to her, she turned and cried out, but not in fear. From behind the dog, a voice answered her, and someone swept past the hound to support and comfort the distressed woman. It should have been her lord, but it was another woman; it was Vail.

They sat among the bodies, because there was no reason to go anywhere else, and talked close together, in words too soft for the hound to hear.

With infinite care, he drew nearer. They were not facing him, and didn't notice it. With each step he altered just slightly the angle of his head, tuning in like an antenna until he could pick up their dialogue, already past its first stage.

"... I couldn't find you again," Vail was saying.

"No matter," the older woman said. "It makes no difference to our fate. I alone ..."

"And I of my kin," added Vail. "We are all that's left, lady."

"You're certain?"

"Certain."

"Where are they?"

"Not here. Wait—" she restrained the woman, "wait a little while, then I'll show you where."

"And the boy? And the Resurrected?" She shuddered deeply; Vail put an arm around her shoulders.

"The Resurrected were my kin, resurrected no more. The boys—there were more than one, lady—I don't know. They were one of the Five Terrors, you know, bringing the Apocalypse."

The woman shook her head, not knowing. "And this—the Great Offering ..." She looked up at the dragon.

Now Vail didn't understand. They didn't share a common mythology.

"And the hound, Gaveral?" Now they both turned, seeing the dog closer to them than they'd supposed, too weary for alarm. "False," the woman moaned bitterly.

"There is another like him," Vail said softly. "I have seen him, inside the castle; but he trails another, not me."

"Who?"

"I don't know. I see him through windows and in distant corners."

The woman and the girl drew closer together and

stared at the dog. The woman's mouth formed silent words. The girl took her hand and whispered into her ear. Even then she was watching the animal.

Suddenly the woman looked hard at Vail and said, "You came from outside, didn't you?" She pulled away and stood up. "Are you a Resurrect?"

"I was Farmhouse Kin," Vail protested.

"Are you sent to kill me?" the woman demanded.

"No! I kill no one. I was sent on this mission, to bring peace to us all."

But the woman was already moving away, stumbling over bodies in her hurry.

"Wait!" Vail called. "I am safe in the hands of my loving God; stay with me! He keeps me safe, so you will be also with me."

The woman paused, looked at the hound already following her, not trusting his purpose. Vail caught up with her. "I know where—" she began, then whispered the rest.

As they passed into the castle, the screen went blank.

| | | | | | | | | | |

Morris let the tape run and run but the picture did not come back. Once there was a fairly long display of what looked like falling snow, or it may just have been some kind of interference. Then blank again. He prowled around the edges of the landscape with eyes hungry for any sign of life within. Vail's confidence in her God's safe hands made him yawn with despair, for there was nothing he could do to save her or to help Sam, pursued by the second hound inside the castle.

This brought him back to the forest side, the hopeless sight of the Westgate barred with creeper and snow. It was the greatest temptation, to stride over the trees and thrust open the gate, to be done with those silly rules, when Patrick was probably about to do that himself.

In a kind of desperate anger, he ventured onto the landscape and crouched down in front of the little door.

It wasn't so very little after all. As in a dream, he almost believed he might worm himself through it; which was ridiculous. He reached out to brush away the creeper. Its scarf of snow was realistically cold.

The creeper was not to be simply brushed aside; it clung to pitted stone and wood as a good parasite should. As Morris tugged at it he felt he was doing the same to strings of tiny suckers in his mind.

The gate was not fastened: he pushed it open. And now he realized he'd had no need to do all that, for he could see easily over the wall into the alleyway. He wished he'd left it alone.

But looking over the top of the wall turned him into a feefifum giant fishing for minnow victims. It was hard to feel benevolent. *I am doing this to help them,* he reminded himself, *to stave off destruction.*

As the alleyway was empty and boring, it was impossible to help anybody, so he stepped over the lower outside wall in order to see into the mysterious Dancing Court. His foot just about slotted into the 191 narrow space: when he brought over the other foot he felt the outer wall begin to cave in. In slight alarm he glanced down and rested his left hand on its top surface. Several small stones tipped off onto his wedged foot; the top layer of snow melted beneath his fingers. He wondered how he was to get back to safety without causing more damage.

But he could see into the fatal courtyard, and as it was a larger area than where he was, he took another step to stand inside it. The mystery object off center *was* a covered well. His back and elbows scraped the castle wall as he bent down. He tried to pry off the cover but it was not to be done. A strap of rusted iron broke away and wouldn't fit back into place. The well was dried up, in any case, and had a faint but unpleasant stench. He wiped his hands on the castle wall, rather than on himself. They left long smears very like giant snail tracks. With luck they would dry and disappear before the God Patrick arrived on the scene.

As he stared at the defaced wall, Morris thought he saw a slight movement from inside the building. He had to press his face against the wall and squint one-eyed through the window, which was not very satisfactory. He began to move slowly, doing this, from one window to the next. The rooms were sparsely furnished: in one he saw a large bed with bright checked covers. In another ... Too late, he realized he'd stepped out of the courtyard across into a much narrower space, and demolished a section of wall in doing so.

He told himself firmly that that was nothing compared with what Patrick meant to do very soon. Also, that Patrick would be interested to learn what Morris had seen; his information would doubtless be useful. Comforted, he continued peering in at every window. The movement he'd thought he'd seen must have been an illusion. The building was empty, at this side at least.

Ah no! An arched window larger than any so far looked down on a chapel, a simple chamber with an altar at one end over which were mounted several great banners, which had been either broken or torn. A silver cup was spilled on the altar, and at its foot lay the bodies of two men, the lord and his brother Highborn.

As Morris gazed, his breath clouded the rough glass window. He rubbed it with his hand, which made it worse. Between misery and anger he pulled his sleeve over his hand and scrubbed again: like brittle spun sugar the glass cracked and jointed inward. Little pieces of it patterned down onto the chapel floor.

A voice in his head, screamed: *What are you doing!*
—*Nothing; gathering useful information.*
You're destroying this fine thing.
—*What fine thing? It's an oversized toy, that's all.*
Destroying it, clumsy idiot.
—*Nothing to what Patrick'll do shortly.*
He'll go mad when he sees.
—*Rubbish; he'll be grateful to me for starting it off for him. It's all dead in there, the game's finished. He hasn't frozen it, he's finished it.*

Stupidly, Morris poked at the spoiled glass so that

another, larger piece bent away from its leading. An inner voice, much smaller than the first, mourned, *I want to go home.*

And where was that?

How long, in their time, had those two bodies lain there? Since they were not real, decaying flesh, it was impossible to know. *Think about that,* Morris lectured himself, *not stupid things like home.* He thought of Vail's watchful, trusting face looking at him.

I am haunted. Love.

20

The small pale face looking up at him from the sad chapel was Sam's, not Vail's. Morris cleared his vision by blinking, as if he'd been crying, which was not true. And there was Sam, gazing up in the old trusty way, waiting for speech. (For a moment, Morris was inside Sam and knew how it felt to be seeing that great face filling all the broken window space.)

It did help, though, to make quiet conversation possible. "Hello," Morris said, "how goes it with you?"

Sam showed no surprise. "Time passes very strangely," he said. "I'm not sure how long I've been in this place."

Morris couldn't enlighten him. "Are you all right?" he asked.

"There has been carnage," Sam said. He indicated the two bodies by the altar.

"I know. The lord and his brother."

"There were children here," Sam told him. He hesitated. "And our people. I saw it happen."

"You must be pleased," Morris suggested. "The castle must belong to you now."

195

"Even so." He failed completely to look joyful.

"Did you find Vail?" Morris asked.

"No, Lord—but she's here, I've trailed her sometimes, but my hound keeps me from her." He glanced behind him with a resignation that turned to disbelief. He spoke to something that Morris couldn't see, then went a moment to investigate for himself, and came back to tell Morris, "The hound, Lord, he's dead. He lies here, suddenly dead. But you knew this?"

"His job's finished," Morris said. It was unpleasantly ominous. He wanted to reach through the broken glass and snatch Sam up in his hand. Which would destroy, not save, him.

The little man was waiting for further orders. In the meantime he set the spilled silver cup upright and smoothed the altar cloth. He threw a torn banner across the two bodies, but didn't care to touch them.

Morris couldn't think of anything to say.

"This place," Sam offered, "is not really as we'd always supposed."

"No?"

"The furniture—" he glanced around, seeing none —"*altogether*, would hardly suffice our people. Not that we could get the massive pieces through our doors." His face twitched at the idea of it. "All these cold empty rooms here," he went on, "and we thought—we'd always believed—"

"It belongs to you now," Morris said.

"So it does. To me alone. I am king. Without even a hound. Lord, what shall I do with it? I'd be happier back home."

There was such pain in the simple statement. Morris said, "So would I." As he said it, it was an absolute truth.

After a long silence, "Shall I go now?" Sam asked.

"Why not? But where are all your people?" Sam shook his head. "What happened to them?"

"I don't know, Lord. Am I king of an empty country, too?"

"Surely not. Go home, Sam."

He looked away from Morris to the bodies on the floor, then back, in some distress. "I forget why I'm here," he cried. "Shall I know how to get out, my way home?"

"Of course," Morris said, "there's nothing to stop you."

"I forget!"

"Look—" Morris deliberately smashed a lower pane of glass—"look, climb up here, get out of this window, then you can find your way around the courtyards to the Westgate—I'll show you where it is." Though Sam looked imploringly at him, he didn't dare take him up in his hand, sure that he'd turn immediately into lifeless plastic.

The little man dragged a stool over to the window, clambered onto it, and hauled himself out of the window. The drop on the other side was quite steep for him, but he knew not to beg Morris's help. When he stood beside his God's foot, not touching it, it was exactly like a scene from Gulliver. Who, Morris recalled, could take much greater liberties with his Lilliputians than he could with Sam or Vail. Not, he also 197 thought he remembered, that it did Gulliver any good, in the end.

"See," he said to Sam, "if you go back the way I came—you can see where I've conveniently knocked a bit of wall down for you—you'll come to the Dancing Court, and then it's easy; the Westgate is open; and you're more or less home." He crouched down, to talk more quietly, and to push over a further section of wall to help Sam.

"That's the way home?" Sam asked. He really didn't remember. Morris thought, *Something's happening to his memory; he must be running down, not frozen but running down.* He ached to pick Sam up and deposit him directly onto his home ground. If he was about to die, he should die there. But Sam had already started out, scrambling over the ruined wall with a ferocity that reminded Morris of the painful way in which the lordly lady had deserted her companions in the secret room.

He stood quite still until Sam had achieved the wall and must by now be in the courtyard. It would be dreadful to step on him, after so much trouble.

With care, he retraced his own steps. Sam was in the Dancing Court, bent double, his head on his knees, near the gate. "Come on," Morris urged him, "don't give up, you're nearly there; just through the little alleyway, and you're home." Sam stared up at him. "Please get up."

It hurt him to watch Sam drag himself across the
yard when perhaps the poor creature was only able

to think: Why doesn't the God help me? He went through into the alleyway and stood leaning against the wall like someone in a daze, not distressed or in a panic any more.

"Go left," Morris told him, "just a few steps, follow the wall, you'll come to the door to the outside."

"Left? Now?"

"Yes, now. Please do it, for my sake."

Sam lifted his head as if he'd forgotten whose sake that was; but obeyed, trailing one hand along the wall, blindly, until he reached the gate.

"There!" Morris cried. "You've made it! Outside, and you'll be able to breathe again, you'll be home!" As if (a last hope) Sam would be all right once in his own environment; a returned fish, a spaceman . . . He willed him every smallest part of the way, through that old doorway, where he tripped over a swag of creeper to land fallen, prone, in the snow. "Get up!" Morris ordered. "You're there! Take a deep breath, Sam, get up!"

After a very long minute, Sam raised his head and peered in front of him at the rising ground and the gaunt trees. It seemed that he did not remember them, and, with an effort far beyond his size, he pulled himself up onto hands and knees, away from the castle and into the forest.

Morris felt like cheering. He really did believe that, between them, they had achieved a great victory. Then he came back to himself with the realization of the damage he'd already caused to the castle, and the 199 fact that he was still wedged in it. He tried, therefore, to extract himself as neatly as possible, demolishing more wall as he did so and making unsightly footprints in the snow on the way out of the landscape. He peered among the trees for a sight of Sam, but he'd disappeared, probably back into his old camouflage. It was a slight comfort only, knowing that Patrick would be back very soon and not at all glad to see that Morris had been trampling over the setup. Nor, probably, that the action hadn't completely stopped, as he'd intended, but had been grinding relentlessly on to its own crumbling doom.

He sat on the floor at the edge of the forest and surveyed it sadly. There was nothing else to do. He thought that the general view looked even more decrepit than it had only a short while ago: surely more of the trees were dead or dying? And the castle itself seemed well on the way to being a ruin; much more so than his few little knocks accounted for. It was frightening, unnerving.

What had happened to the other hound, the false Gaveral? Still trailing Vail and the lady? Or as dead as the hound in the chapel? (He told himself crossly: *run down, not dead,* but it wouldn't do). He roused himself to go to the console to try the monitor, just in case ... with the familiar series of jazzed images, blurred fogs, and complete blanks. He tried a second switch and ran the tape at speed for a couple of minutes, till a sudden true picture arrested him. Playing it correctly, he found himself watching Sam, wandering along a dark passageway. At a door, he stopped and turned to question his tracker, with something of a smile, as if they'd become friends. Then Sam went on, coming shortly into the chapel where Morris had seen him last. It looked quite a spacious place, seen this way.

Sam crossed to examine the two bodies by the altar, but as Morris had noticed, he didn't touch them. When he straightened up, he turned again to the hound, with an immensely sad expression. He spoke to the dog, but the words were unclear. Then there was a sudden darkening, as of a blind being lowered, and a sound of breaking glass. The hound swayed its head to see lumps of glass showering the floor and a giant, moonlike face looming in at the window. It was a profound shock to see himself through their eyes.

The hound must have drawn back out of sight, because there was Sam once more, gazing upward and, after a lapse of memory, recognizing his Lord. His look of welcome and relief also pained Morris to the heart; it filled the screen almost tangibly. (How long had he wandered through that hopeless place on his God's work? Gradually losing sight of his purpose, finding no victory, no reunion.)

Now Morris watched again the little scene where Sam tidied the altar and covered the bodies, in respect. He could see in closeup how relief was quite quickly giving way to puzzlement, from puzzlement to the beginnings of pain and atrophy. When Sam finally cried, "Shall I know how to get out, my way home?" Morris was overwhelmed with such remorse that he knew that complete loss. It was only then that the picture faded, as if the hound had endured longer than Sam had believed, also faithful to his task beyond the limit.

Morris stared at the blank screen; and stared; at nothing.

21

t may have been a long time, or no time at all, until Morris knew that Patrick and Ian were in the room with him, not noticing his silly state because they were too busy discussing the fine details of the final onslaught. Ian appeared to have surrendered hope of avoiding it any longer and was putting his mind to the technicalities.

"Hello again," Patrick said jauntily. "Everything all right?"

Morris pulled a funny face and stepped smartly away from his own recent disaster area. "I don't think the program *stopped* exactly," he said.

"No?" Patrick glanced with suspicion between Morris, Ian, and the castle, considering who to blame. "Why do you say that?"

"I think it's still been running—only, not right," Morris said. "Sort of running *down*. As if it's just going to crumble to its end." *With luck he'll accept the damage I did as general decay.*

Ian was already scanning the console. "Idiot," he said to Patrick, "you did it wrong. Look here, you've—"

"Then you told me wrong," Patrick objected. "I followed your instructions exactly—straight away—Morris'll tell you—and now look at it!"

Ian took no notice. He set about trying to put all to rights, with the warning: "It can't be done. Poor old thing's at its last gasp. What a waste." He gave it up and turned to Patrick, who was still ranting privately on the boundary.

He called Ian a few choice names and strode away from him, glaring at the decaying landscape all the while. "And how did those happen?" he said suddenly.

Morris's heart dropped.

"What?" Ian asked.

Patrick pointed. "Those. Giant footprints in the snow." He glared at Morris. "Who's been knocking my castle down?" he demanded.

It sounded so like the Three Bears that Morris had to swallow a hysterical giggle.

Ian said, "It wouldn't have made any difference, Patrick. You twiddled the wrong knobs."

Patrick looked as if he was going to knock Ian down.

"Look," Ian said dangerously, "I'm standing on the setup, right in front of the castle gates." Which he did, never taking his eyes from Patrick. "Look," he went on, "I'm touching the wall," feeling backward with one hand.

At only a gentle touch, several stones were dislodged from the top of the wall, to fall without a sound.

"Get off there," Patrick threatened.

Ian dared to look away, over the wall into the courtyard. "It's still there," he said with interest, "the old Trojan dragon thing; it's still there, come and see."

"If I do, I'm going to—"

"And little dead bodies, all around. Come and see."

Patrick deliberately kicked a tree as he did so, to show he was God. Morris wondered if he too would be allowed to join in. He thought he'd better wait.

After peering gloomily over the wall, Patrick reached in and picked up one of the little figures. He examined it with some care, stiffened his hand as if to crush it, then tossed it to Morris, saying, "You can have this if you want. Souvenir."

The poor thing fell short. Morris stepped onto the setup to retrieve it. Patrick didn't growl at him.

The figure was just a colorless games piece, well made, lying on its side in an attitude of sleep or death. By some cunning technology, it had previously moved about, upright, and perhaps it had even appeared to speak and think. Which it hadn't, of course. Though he didn't really want it, he thought it might be interesting to take apart some time, maybe find out how it worked; so he put it in his pocket. Then he continued to stand idle while the two gods bickered and knocked bits off the once-beautiful landscape.

"Why don't you try the handbook?" Morris asked when he was tired of their play.

The gods fell silent, and looked at him.

He repeated his question.

205

Ian at least was interested. "It's an idea," he said.

Patrick sneered. "Fairy tales? That book alone cost more than—" he stove the main gates in with a single vicious kick—"and for what? A great long list of highly expensive components and a load of fairy tales."

Ian was already searching for the book. "Programs," he corrected Patrick, "not fairy tales. If you know how to interpret them they supply all the answers. Perhaps we can still—" He found the book and took it over to the light, turning pages rapidly.

Patrick willfully snapped off a piece of turret. "I tell you what," he said, "the next thing I set up here's going to be a lot simpler than this. Pure landscape, or a maze—I've been thinking about that one; how about a gigantic maze on a proper grid, but more or less flat, none of this—"

Morris glanced at Ian and saw how the new idea had caught his imagination, even as he tried to find another solution to their present problem. He said, "But we tried a maze incorporated into that other setup—what was it—"

"Incorporated," Patrick scoffed, "that's no good; what we want is the whole thing, something we can alter and adapt to different game levels."

Morris interrupted, "This one isn't finished yet!"

Patrick gazed at him as if from another dimension. The reminder sent Ian back into the handbook.

"We could blow it up," Patrick said. He was now in a hurry to start on the new idea.

206 "I thought you wanted to see inside it," Morris said.

"So I did, but that was when it was still a working model. Waste of time." He clipped off a bit more turret. "How do we blow it up, Ian?"

"And this house with it?"

"Oh, give me that damned handbook!"

"Wait—" Ian lifted a hand to stop Patrick. "Here, this is it, I think." He read aloud: " '*Statement*: When all is both lost and fulfilled, then shall the Apocalypse come.' " He glanced up. "I take that to mean when the castle's been taken and the whole campaign finalized."

"Go on."

Ian read on: " 'When God has voided this world, another world shall be created from its foundations and its people shall arise from their sleep to live again.' "

Patrick leaned over and picked up one of the corpses from the courtyard. He studied it. "It's only a way to get you to go on buying their rotten components," he said. "Clever bastards. And does the book say," he asked Ian, "exactly *how* the gods, meaning us, void this world?"

"Hang on. You know none of this text is straightforward."

"If we blow it up," Patrick said, "then we blow up all the little people with it. All right. Here, Morris, come and extract all the bodies you can find. I tell you what, Ian; I'm going to get a much-needed drink, and if you've not found the supposed correct solution by then, I'm taking a sledgehammer to it."

Ian muttered something, not listening.   207

Morris knew this was his last chance to find and

rescue Sam and Vail for himself. And no, the word rescue was false, he admitted, because whatever life they might have had in their own land would drain from them as soon as he picked them up.

They would be two little inert models, like the one now in his pocket.

He hesitated, looked over the castle wall, and asked Ian, "Can I make the hole in the gate bigger, do you think?"

"Why not?" Ian didn't even glance up, on the track of the final mystery, the mythical Apocalypse. He turned his back on Morris to deal with technology.

The gates were of undoubted wood: Morris picked a splinter from his hand. Feeling around, he decided Patrick wouldn't want to reuse the Dragon Carriage, so pushed it aside. The several corpses around it he removed onto the ground outside. None of them were even kin to Vail or Sam, he was sure.

He found a few more figures scattered around, then went to retrieve those in the chapel. Certainly the castle lord and his brother Highborn ought to be given the chance of another life.

To reach them Morris had to smash the chapel window completely. It made an ugly, real sound in an unreal happening. Ian didn't appear to have heard anything.

The two figures were just as all the rest; colorless, interestingly made, slightly sad. It was difficult to tell which was which; all their lively character was quite drained away. Morris thought he might have to pocket one, or both, but shuddered and put them quickly down. Finally, there was the hound, still on guard. Morris touched it with the tip of one finger; then reached in and picked it up. Its eyes were wide open, with a strange depth. He stroked its head but couldn't feel the hidden camera. With a kind of sorry affection, he placed it beside the two brothers. *Now*, he thought, *that's it, unless I can get my great arm inside the very castle. Where she is.*

But no; think again; what about Sam, who had escaped among the trees?

Leave her? Not even try to find her? Oh, but it was impossible to worm into that place, to hook her out, to finally admit that she was never what he had supposed.

Morris began to poke among the trees for Sam. He might or he might not have reached his little forest hut, which was already almost a ruin, its roof stove in by a fallen tree. Morris shifted the tree aside and inserted his fingers into the cavity of the building. To feel that little body, so cold and hard, was physically unpleasant; like discovering a petrified insect in a much dipped-in bag of sweets. When he looked at it, flat on his palm, he found he couldn't believe that *that* had very recently been Sam, his gallant friend.

Friend nearly finished him. He fished in his pocket, cast out the unwanted, meaningless figure, and put Sam gently in its place. Sam belonged, and was going home with him—not to be callously dissected. To be treasured. Vail, on the other hand . . .

Ian said, "Are you finished, Morris? I think I've

worked out what to do, or something anyway. When Patrick comes back."

Morris stepped off the setup. He observed, "It doesn't look as if it'll take much to demolish this lot."

"No. You're right. It's a shame. But the whole thing's only a license to spend money, buy this, add that, you've no idea—" His gaze drifted. "Really, the maze idea could be something, better than all this Disneyland stuff."

Morris said, "I thought it was great. A real world."

"Too real. You have to guard against that."

"I know."

"Stick to board games."

"I know." Morris thought suddenly of his parents. They used to buy a new board game every Christmas, always hopeful, and end up round a tatty old thing they'd played since the dawn of memory. It felt very like time to be getting home. This place—all these houses: Patrick's, Bea's, Ian's—all felt positively alien, and all the people too, however interesting. He said, "I wish this—" he waved at the castle—"wasn't so horribly gloomy."

"Well," Ian said, "with a bit of luck, it might not be. If I've translated myth into program correctly. And here, on cue, is the Great God himself."

"Well," Patrick wanted to know, "are we all ready?"

"Hope so," Ian said. "But don't blame me if it turns out unexpected."

He set something in motion.

210   "Do we all stand well back?" Morris asked, doing so.

"It might be an idea."

Patrick took a number of quick paces up and down, estimating the best view. "I shall charge house repairs up to you, Ian," he said. Ian just about contrived a grin. "How long's this going to take?"

"A few minutes, possibly."

"Are we getting it on video?"

"Sure. Nothing yet."

"Ian, if this is a have-on—"

"Ssh!"

From deep within the castle there came the sound of a low uneven vibration. The three watched, not knowing exactly where to look or what to expect.

"It's purring," Morris said.

The sound steadied and became perhaps a little louder.

Nothing else happened. Patrick plainly wanted to step over the boundary and poke about, to encourage it a little. He nervously advanced and retreated several times, like someone new to a dance routine.

Morris felt in his pocket for Sam and cradled him there. Perhaps it was possible to imagine that he was growing warmer, more "plastic." *Don't be frightened*, went the message to his finger ends.

"It's taking a long time to wind up," Patrick observed. "I don't think you'd any more idea of how to set this up than—than Morris has."

"Possibly," Ian agreed. "I think—"

The Apocalypse began.

It all happened so fast and all before their astonished gaze; first the ground floor was revealed, the massive halls opened to the daylight, then, in se- 211 quence, layer below layer, each floor opened its smooth trapmouth to show the rooms beneath, with lights coming on, white and gold, picking out all the beautiful detail.

As the three ventured close to stare in wonder, Ian said, "It ought to play music!" and, perfectly on cue, so it did; the far-off tinny strains of the long-lost band, playing from nowhere and everywhere, a rousing medieval call to celebration.

"Where are they?" Morris leaned even closer, trying to see the ghostly players as the sound grew louder.

There wasn't even time to cry, Look out! From the very depths of the castle, from its core, a marvelous fountain swam into the light; not water, but swarms of shining particles, color upon color, projected into the air high above their heads, to flutter down like sycamore seeds. Among them were other things— fragments of silk, stars that drifted sideways, white banners so narrow and light that they held up in the air, displaying messages written in fine gold in different languages.

| | | | | | | | | | | |

They stood, stunned. Covered in glory, and very much more.

The wonderful display ended. All was still.

Patrick said, at last, "No, I can't." He held a banner looped between his hands. "It's too much."

Morris asked, dazed, "What does it mean?"

212   "Who knows." Patrick peered, with caution, into

the crater. "But I think I need refreshment, and a bit of meditation." He read the message on the banner, which he didn't understand. "They must," he said, "distribute these things worldwide. And expect the same results." He let it fall fluttering to the ground.

"This one," Ian said, picking up another banner, "is in Latin. It's a bit like the Creed—*et resurrexit . . . secundum scripturas* . . . resurrected according to the scriptures—you see how well educated I am."

Patrick made a feeble raspberry. "Well, it resurrected all right, I'll say that. Come away, Ian, leave it. Morris, you're covered in confetti like a great bridesmaid. Morris, are you deaf?"

"In a minute." He shook his hands gently to see a host of tiny stars glitter from his fingers to the ground.

"Hopeless, the lad's hopeless," Patrick murmured.

They left him, the door open, expecting his "in a minute" to be taken literally. "Well, Ian," Patrick said, "we did a fine job there. Mind you, one or two tersely-worded suggestions to the manufacturers and suppliers won't come amiss. You're good at stern letters—we'll do that tomorrow, then we can get down to this new project . . ."

Ian was heard to mention Christmas Day, when he would be doing other things.

Patrick laughed, having heard all that before. "Don't be long, Morris!" he shouted up the stairwell.

"I won't!"

No, it needed just a few minutes, a last look at what had been; a funny, sad entrancement. Goodbye had to be said, because Vail was still in there somewhere. And considering it, he was glad, because the Last Judgment had been so grand and he was sure she'd witnessed and enjoyed it.

Reason reared its dreary head to sneer and say how stupid and childish that was.

No it wasn't. She was there, she was real, she was truth.

Before he finally left the room (it was a room, now) he sifted through a handful of silken ribbons, half expecting to find a fortune-cookie motto or two for future use round the family table. Some were written in Eastern characters he couldn't even begin to read. One said: AMOR VINCIT OMNIA, which he was sure was Latin again.

He turned it over, and on the reverse side was written the translation: LOVE CONQUERS ALL.

He tossed all the ribbons into the air with the final challenge: "All right—prove it!"